Chapter 1

I SABELLA BALFOUR EMERGED ONSTAGE from the dim wings, hands fluttering as she stepped lively. She scanned the audience, including the nearest box seats, blinking against the brightness of the room. Above her, a gentleman shifted, his earnest gaze following her as she carried a letter over to Mary. Cupping her hand near Mary's ear, Isi stood on tiptoe and whispered, "Isn't this a dream?"

Mary giggled and took the paper. Turning to the audience, she opened it and pretended to read a note from her lover.

"The duke asks me to elope to Gretna Green with him." She spoke with perfect enunciation from the diaphragm, projecting out to the three thousand people sitting before them.

Isi blinked, her heart pounding. She was on stage at Drury Lane. A tingle swirled through her. "A duke who needs to elope to marry? Are you certain he's a duke?" The audience chuckled, knowing the duke was a tailor borrowing a duke's clothing without permission.

Mary threw her arms up in the air and shouted, "Of course he is! Only a duke could win my heart." She waltzed to the desk, pantomimed writing something, and handed Isi back the paper. "Take this to him and tell him I'll meet him there."

Isi scurried off stage. She dreamed of being a leading lady like Mrs. Siddons, but for comedy instead of tragedy. Isi didn't have the stomach for tragedy. She much preferred making people laugh.

Mary's voice floated out with power, and Isi heard a hush descend over the auditorium.

"The audience tonight seems captivated, for once," said Connor. He leaned on a suspended rope.

"Plenty of them are chatting with their neighbors, but we have the attention of some box seats."

She moved further backstage until she found her father sprawled on the floor, his head propped up against the wall, mouth gaping. He'd fallen into his cups before the curtain even rose. Three acts in he was drunk as a wheelbarrow, which she needed if she had any hope of getting him home. Isi crinkled her nose at his stench, a mix of sweat and gin.

"Isi, isn't your next cue coming up?" asked David Martin, the leader of the troupe and her father's best friend from childhood.

The words emanating from the stage floated back to her. He was right.

"I'll try to get him conscious by the end of the play." David crossed his arms and cleared his throat, his tone gruff.

She placed a chaste kiss on his scruffy cheek to thank him. He patted her head and waved her away. A pang tore at her chest, and she wished her own father paid such attention to her.

Isi paced near the edge of the stage until Mary called for her maid, her voice shrill. With her thoughts still on her father, she escaped the dim wings. Wringing her hands, she channeled her worry for Papa into her performance. A lady's maid had a right to worry when her employer flouted the rules of society.

She tallied in her mind the cost of a hackney home. Fighting a grimace at the total, she delivered her lines and pranced around without thought, grateful for hours spent rehearsing.

The gentle rumble of conversation from the audience drew Isi's attention back to the present. Her heart raced, and she turned to hide a smile that was not part of the play. She was performing at Drury Lane. Her excitement thrummed in her chest.

2

After delivering her last lines, she hurried to change before setting off to discover if David had roused her father.

Grasping her wool shawl to keep the chill off, she opened the back door to the theatre. Just outside, she heard a man sputtering and splashing. Dark shadows enveloped the alley. Squinting, Isi wished for a candle or a streetlamp.

"Papa?"

"He's here, Isi." Another splash, and David pulled papa over to the door, which she swung wide.

Water dripped from his sopping hair into red-rimmed eyes. Mouth agape, he looked like a caught fish gasping for air.

"Is your part done?"

She shut the door to keep the chill night air out and nodded as David slapped her father on the back, sending him sprawling toward a small three-legged wooden stool.

"Take him home and tell him to meet me in the morning. Make sure he's awake before noon. We have things that need discussing."

"Please don't turn us out, we have nowhere to go, and I belong on stage—" David held up a hand.

"You'll always have a place here, Isi. But him—?" He glanced at her father, his cheeks drooping, his eyes large and glistening. "He needs to pull himself together. Last week, he messed up the timing on the curtain, and the audience glimpsed us setting the stage."

Isi hung her head. He was right. Performances depended on everyone doing their part, both on and off the stage. If the curtains fell before Mary finished her soliloquy or Isi blundered on stage before her time, the illusion broke. People only recalled the spectacle.

With a sigh, she glanced over her shoulder at her father, who had fallen asleep again, his cheek squished against the wall. She would haul him home later. Perhaps Connor could help him into a carriage after the show. He couldn't walk back to their rooms, not as wet as he was. In the cool night air of early March, he'd catch a cold. Mary's melodious voice beckoned Isi to view her performance from the wings, carrying her away from her worries, if only for the moment.

Chapter 2

I N THE THEATRE ROYAL Drury Lane auditorium the scent of oranges mingled with the warm air. Candles flickered in large chandeliers, reflecting off mirrors and flooding the room with light. Jonathan Sterling, Duke of Edston, almost smiled.

"What does she think she's doing? Prancing around the stage as though she were a fairy instead of a lady's maid. If my abigail did such a thing, I'd pack her off right away."

Jonathan grunted at Miss Gibbon's comment. The woman talked in a continual stream. Her tone and speed seldom varied from a monotonous monologue with nary a breath.

He was enjoying the show. The one onstage, not the performance Miss Gibbon was putting on. Theatre was an uncommon interest among his peers, but a well-produced play never failed to stir him.

In his box just above the stage, he leaned closer to the railing, squinting at the girl to whom Miss Gibbon referred.

She did flit around, but he narrowed his eyes, scrutinizing her. Did her energy come from nerves or an exuberance for the performance?

When a play drew him in, he sometimes imagined himself on stage, acting. But then he'd picture his peers throwing fruit and laughing. A duke had a part to play, expectations to meet.

Like a rotten tomato, Miss Gibbon's voice assailed him again. "—to visit with Mrs. Drew and her son after. I believe you know him. He's—"

"I know Mr. Drew, but I have no interest in joining them tonight. In fact, I am engaged after the performance." He wasn't. But after attending the theatre, he reveled in a quiet evening to think over the aspects of the play he'd enjoyed. Quiet was not a word used to describe Miss Gibbon. "Perhaps Mr. Drew and his mother might escort you and Mrs. Gibbon home?"

"I suppose we might enquire at the break." Miss Gibbon opened her small ivory fan, fluttering it near her face and glancing at her mother, who sat in a chair just behind them, speaking with one of her friends who'd come to join them in his box.

The cloying scent of roses slipped along the light breeze toward him. "Yes, lets. I'm sure Mr. Drew won't mind, and you may discover his opinion of the dancing girl."

"She does sort of float over the stage like a ballerina or something, doesn't she?" Miss Gibbon prattled on, and Jonathan leaned forward in his seat, tuning her out to enjoy the performance.

When possible, he avoided spending time with her. Mother had invited her before begging off because of a headache. His mother approved of Miss Gibbon as a potential match for Jonathan, hoping he would choose her to take over as Duchess of Edston now that his father had passed.

But the idea of ignoring her constant diatribe on society and the flow of gossip about their acquaintances fatigued him more than a day spent touring his extensive estate in Yorkshire.

The girl on stage grinned, hiding her face from most of the audience. He had his answer. She enjoyed acting—her flighty manner was not nerves but an overabundance of energy.

After the play ended, he handed Mrs. and Miss Gibbon off to Mr. Drew and his aging mother, who wore too many ostrich feathers in her hair. She kept brushing them out of her eyes, and he wondered why she'd chosen such a ridiculous headdress for the theatre. They blocked her view as well as those behind her.

Jonathan hovered near the stage door. He jiggled the knob, glad to find it open. With one last glance at the crowds full of their own self-importance, he slipped inside.In front of him, a woman packed costume pieces in a trunk. Jonathan spun away from two men carrying a desk off stage. Another man coiled a rope, casting him a glance.

No polished wood or brass fixtures adorned the space. To his right sat a jumbled assortment of furniture. A back corner reminded him of his mother's dressing room before a ball, gowns, gloves, and hats spilling out on tables and chairs.

He caught sight of the girl behind an armoire overflowing with lavish costumes, her arms supporting a grey-haired man swaying on his feet. She pulled one of his arms over her shoulder, flailing as they both leaned back too far.

Hurrying over, he wrapped his arm about the man, who smelled like a distillery. She grunted, and they lowered him onto the stool. "Best to leave him there. He won't notice," said Jonathan, swiping at the dampness the man had left behind on his sleeve.

"But everyone else will," she muttered, heaving a sigh. The woman tore her expression from the older man, wringing her hands. "I'm sorry. I don't know you."

He blinked and realized he hadn't introduced himself. "Jonathan Sterling, Duke of Edston."

"Your Grace." She bobbed a curtsy, ducking her head. "I'm Isabella Courteney. Are you searching for someone?"

He nodded and swallowed. "You."

She tilted her face up. Her green eyes and auburn hair shimmered, and a smile tugged at the corners of her full lips.

"Me?" Glancing at the people cleaning up the props nearby, she lowered her voice. "Why?"

"I wished to compliment you on your performance."

She blinked quickly in surprise, her eyelashes fluttering. "I thank you. But my part was rather minor. Are you certain you are not looking for Miss Mary Robinson? She performed the lead this evening." Miss Courteney leaned to the side to search behind him, presumably for Miss Robinson.

"She gave a fine performance as well. But the exuberance you brought to the part of the maid was quite entertaining." He watched as she met his gaze for a moment before staring down at their feet. He couldn't be certain, but he wondered if she blushed beneath her stage make up.

"What gave you the inspiration to play the maid in such a spirited manner? Was the part written that way?"

She definitely blushed now.

A grin spread over his face and a pleasant warmth course through him. Most women of his acquaintance wielded blushes as weapons. To find one who could act, yet wore her true emotions on display for all to see was refreshing.

When her eyes met his again, the blush faded and she raised one eyebrow.

"There was little direction for the part. Given such an opportunity, I could interpret her motives and lines as I pleased."

She gave the maid motives? That she put such effort into what she called a minor part intrigued him further. Her passion for acting on the stage was more than just a means of income for her.

Envy filled him, irrational as it was. Here was a woman who enjoyed her work enough that she happily expended extra effort in accomplishing it. She glowed with delight at his compliment on her performance and the radiance of her joy drew him in. He took another step toward her. His voice was low and husky when he said, "I'd like to become your patron." He'd thought this through while Miss Gibbon had talked over the performance. He admired Miss Courteney. Assisting her career appealed to him.

The woman slapped him. "I'm not that kind of actress."

His cheek stung, and a flush crept up his neck. The bustling behind him stopped. He cringed when she said, "I won't play your mistress for any amount of money."

He clapped a hand on his face. "I didn't—I don't—"

"Others may not find shame in such an arrangement, but I do. And to make the offer in front of my father!" Her lips curled, eyes narrowing. She gestured at the unconscious man on the stool, drool dripping onto his chest.

He stepped back. "That is not what I meant." He straightened, lowering his hand from his face, his cheek still stinging.

She pursed her lips, and her eyes looked prepared to shoot arrows at him.

"I am a gentleman, miss. I only came to inquire—that is, to offer to be your patron because I enjoyed your performance. For you to accuse me of anything else with no foundation on which to base your claims is outrageous." She opened her mouth, but he ignored her. Turning, he fled the room, ignoring the looks thrown his way.

A mistress indeed. He might laugh at the misunderstanding in the morning and attend the next performance when a new production began, but he doubted it.

Chapter 3

THE MOST NOBLE DUKE of Edston. How dare he assume if he threw money at her, she would accept it without giving him a piece of her mind. If his proposal were so honorable, why had his cheeks flushed? His running away also indicated guilt, didn't it? What a lecherous, wealthy rake!

She stumbled over the cobblestones, the weight of her father almost sending her to her knees. His arm slipped until she shrugged it back up across her shoulders. She pressed on. A snore in her ear made her groan in frustration. She jerked her elbow into his ribs. His coughing fit almost toppled them both.

Their rooms were too far away for her to carry him. She arched her neck over his arm, looking behind her for a hackney. They had not yet left sight of the theatre, and one carriage stood in front of the building. Squinting against the encroaching darkness, she just made out the license number painted on the side of the vehicle.

With a sigh of relief, she turned, hobbling toward the carriage. "Excuse me, sir." The driver patted the horse's nose and turned to face her.

"Would you be available for hire?"

The man nodded, fluffing his mustache with a huff of air she could see. Despite the slightly warmer days, nights were still cold enough to see one's breath.

Isi's shoulders sagged as she waddled her father around the side and waited for the driver to open the door.

She shoved Papa inside. The cold latched onto her now that the heat from his body was gone. He slumped on the forward-facing seat, so she sat on the other. The ride would put a dent in what they'd earned that evening, but it was worth every shilling. Soon they'd be back in their rooms and she could curl up under her blankets and sleep.

She wished she could keep Papa from drinking. Sober, he was caring and a hard worker. But since Mother had passed away four years ago, he'd been soaking himself into a stupor every night.

The sound of the horse's hooves clopping on the cobblestones lulled her into a daze, and she startled when the carriage came to a halt, swaying. Papa snorted but didn't wake.

She pushed him out the door and watched a puff of dust rise around him as his body thumped to the ground. Holding on to the door frame, she hopped out and removed the coins from her purse to pay the driver.

As the horses pulled away, Isi nudged her father. He groaned, unmoving.

Her arms protested, but she shoved him into a sitting position. She hauled a bucketful of water from the horse trough toward papa and threw the contents in his face.

He spluttered, straightening. "Is it over?"

"Yes. We're home, Papa. I can't get you upstairs on my own."

He smiled up at her, his eyes still glazed over. "My sweet child." His stringy hair dripped, but she didn't correct him. Sweet was the last word that described her tonight.

"Let's go." She swung the door open and gestured through the hall and up the stairs.

Rolling over, he pushed himself up and swayed on his feet. She hurried to steady him and gave him a gentle push inside.

The space was dark but familiar. The acrid smell of tallow candles permeated the peeling wallpaper. She took three strides, then maneuvered around the small table, holding her breath.

With every creak of the wooden floorboards, she grimaced and wished Papa would take care to make his steps lighter.

As they reached the landing, a light appeared behind her at the bottom of the stairs. "Is that you, Miss Courteney?"

"Yes, Mrs. Pitt."

"Just getting in?"

"Yes." She leaned around Papa and opened the door to his room.

Below, their landlady harrumphed. "You haven't forgotten rent is due?"

"No. I have not forgotten. But as it is so late, perhaps such business might wait until tomorrow." She shoved against his back, and he trudged inside, leaning forward until she thought he would fall. And he did, sending a shudder through his bed frame. With a sigh of relief that the task of caring for him was over for the evening, she straightened and rolled her neck, trying to relieve some tension.

"Fine. Tomorrow. I'll not be put off. If I don't have that money by dinnertime, you'll both be out on your—"

"Yes, thank you. Good night, Mrs. Pitt." Isi hung her head and went into her room. She should wash and change, but her eyes were already closed, and the effort to open them, fetch water, and undress were too much.

Besides, there was no sense lighting a candle. It would only disturb the other creepy crawly tenants.

Shuffling forward, she reached up, removing pins from her hair. Eyes still closed, she placed them on the edge of the table beside the empty wash basin.

She stepped once more, her knee just brushing the thin coverlet hanging off her bed. Sinking beneath the covers, she curled in a ball in the sagging middle. The ropes needed tightening again. She breathed in the musty straw-filled tick.

Perhaps she had been too hasty in rejecting the duke's proposal

More money would be nice. She imagined a second chaff-filled mattress. But at what cost? The duke claimed he didn't want a mistress.

But why would he offer to be her patron? Unless he saw potential in her?

She recalled the way he'd stood with such a commanding air, yet spoken softly.

But there was something about him. A gentleness in his face that didn't match the set of his broad shoulders, which, she'd noted, filled out his coat nicely. His tailor was a talented man, knowing just how to show his grace's physique to its best advantage.

Still, handsome or not, he did not have the right to make requests with no thought to how it might affect others.

Her feet aching from supporting the weight of two people, she lay awake pondering the duke's offer. By sunrise, her muddled mind still fantasizing about the Most Noble Duke of Edston, she concluded she may have been hasty in her refusal of the man's offer.

Chapter 4

THE DAY AFTER HIS humiliation at the theatre, Jonathan stood before his valet, dressing for a ride in the park. A knock sounded at his dressing room door.

"Enter," he said over Barkley's balding head as the man brushed down his shirt.

The door creaked open, and the butler appeared. "A young lady requests a meeting, Your Grace. I told her you were not home for visitors, but she insists on speaking with you."

He shook his head, intending to send the girl away. "Does she have a card?"

"No, sir. The name she gave is Miss Isabella Courteney."

His face froze, then warmed, jaw dropping. Barkley's hands froze around the stiff cravat. The man peered up. "Are you well, Your Grace? Perhaps if—"

"I'm fine, Barkley." To the butler he said, "I will be down in a moment. Show her to the parlor and offer her tea."

"Yes, Your Grace." The butler nodded and left.

Jonathan cleared his throat and motioned for Barkley to finish dressing him.

Why had Miss Courteney sought him out at home? Had she come alone? There'd been no mention of anyone else.

His palms began to sweat, and he stretched his fingers taut, flexing them even as he stood still so Barkley could tie his neckcloth.

She had already humiliated him in public. Was she back for another round? Her fiery temper from the night before indicated she was not one to shy away from confrontation. She'd struck him with no thought to the consequences.

An image of her face flashed before him then. Her lips in a frown, almost pouting, her eyes blazing, her determination to stand up to him despite his higher station. He admired her courage. Coming to his home was another act of courage. He was curious as to her motives for this visit.

Ten minutes later, he descended the stairs from the upper floor of the townhouse to ground level. Outside the parlor, he took a deep breath before opening the door.

As he entered, it became immediately apparent that Miss Courteney was beautiful in any light, be it warm sunshine or the flickering glow of candlelight. Her copper hair shined in the sunlight streaming through the windows, and she cut a fine figure in her dress, which was fashionable but not as elegant as those favored by the *ton*.

A quick glance around revealed no one else, so he pushed the door wide and stepped over to a blue velvet armchair near the empty fireplace, keeping several paces away from her. "Please, sit." He gestured to a matching settee across from him in front of the window. Her hair shimmered in the light as she sat. Once she settled, he lowered into his seat. Where was Mother? To be alone with an actress...word would spread faster than a fire in a field during a dry spell.

"To what do I owe this visit?" Had she come to berate him again? "I assumed we would avoid each other. After last night's...unpleasantness."

She glanced at her folded hands, yellow kid gloves stretching taut as her fingers tightened. "I am sorry for my behavior. It was a shock to be approached by someone of your station."

"Forgive me for that. I know we had not been introduced." He'd thought up a dozen different, more proper scenarios to the one he'd enacted. Acceptable alternatives such as finding an acquaintance to introduce them or telling the theatre manager that he sought a chaperoned audience with her.

But he could no more change his actions than he could turn her into the next Duchess of Edston.

"No need to apologize, Your Grace. You offered to be my patron. I suppose I read too much into such an overture. I was tired, and you were a stranger. And Papa—well, it was up to me to get him home."

"I should have hired the two of you a carriage."

She waved a hand. "It was not your concern." Her brow knit, and she fiddled with her gloves.

The woman before him stood in contrast to happy young woman she'd been the night before. Remembering the way she had danced across the stage, exuding happiness, warmed his heart. Though she appeared just as pretty off stage as on, with her creamy skin and the sheen to her copper hair, her downcast expression added a maturity she'd not worn during her performance. Forcing such thoughts away, he reminded himself that while it was acceptable to profess an appreciation of the arts, society showed their love through money. He longed to take her hands in his to stop their fidgeting, to smooth her wrinkled brow and bring a smile to her face that he was sure would put the sun to shame. But he had his place in the world, and she had hers.

His duty was to make a suitable match and produce an heir for the family's title. That meant marrying Miss Gibbon or one of the other women his mother paraded before him, a lady groomed for such a position. Well-bred young ladies with family titles and fortunes that dated back centuries.

After a few minutes, the silence became unbearable. She needed to leave before he did something foolish and ruined both their reputations. "Was there another reason for your visit this afternoon?"

"I wondered if your offer to stand as my patron—that is, if you might still consider—" With a frustrated huff, she pounded on her knees and leveled him with her sharp gaze. "I was wondering if you would still be my patron."

He cupped his chin and considered her request. "What changed your mind?" He needed to buy himself time before answering her.

His infatuation with the lovely actress had felt harmless the previous evening. Now, even he questioned his motives, and if he didn't know his own mind, the *ton* would decide it for him.

Her shoulders fell. "I do not earn enough in the roles I am playing. I hope that having a patron may help me get more prominent parts in upcoming productions."

Jonathan rubbed the smooth skin of his chin. She wanted his money, but only to help her work harder and earn more money on her own skill. Her determination to strive for what she wished was an admirable quality. But if he sponsored her, everything would have to appear as legitimate and above board as it would be. "What is in it for me?"

She straightened, and her eyes blazed with fire again. "I thought you said—"

"Not that," he interjected, feeling his cheeks warm. "I mean, if I am to be your patron, are your intentions to stay with your current company? I only worry that my endorsement carries weight, and I won't support an actress who accepts risqué parts."

"You care what people think of you?"

"Yes, of course. Or what they think of my reputation."

"Reputation. Just another word for a façade. A persona you show the world. You are not so different from us actors, but at least we can differentiate masks from reality."

Jonathan shifted in his seat but didn't take his eyes off the woman. Her piercing gaze made his scalp prickle, and a cold pit formed in his stomach. He forced himself to look away. "I do not wish to hold you back, but rather to hold you to a higher standard and to help you achieve your potential."

"Who gets final say, Your Grace?" she added after a moment, as though reminding herself to whom she spoke.

"I think the troupe leader has that ability, does he not?" He studied her, searching for one minor detail on which to fixate. If he found a flaw, he might ignore the uncomfortable feelings stirring inside his chest. She lacked freckles. Her angular nose accentuated high cheekbones which framed glowing green eyes. Even her ears were an appropriate size.

Her lips tightened, drawing his attention. Even twisted in displeasure, her mouth was full and a lovely light pink. "It would be easy for you to throw money his way and guarantee I either do or don't get a part."

Exasperated at her mistrust and flawless appearance, he held out his hands and said, "Fine. I will leave those decisions up to the troupe leader and you. Heaven forbid my opinion carry any weight." He waited for her reply and decided her flaws were internal. She was stubborn, jumped to conclusions, and had come to meet with him alone, which suggested she was not as concerned for her reputation as she claimed. However, he supposed she wanted to keep her financial affairs private.

After a few moments, she gave one firm nod.

"Perfect." He stood. "Thank you for coming. I look forward to seeing what your troupe puts together next." His mother would faint if she were to discover how often this girl had occupied his thoughts since last night. "Will they still be at Drury Lane?"

"Yes, we are preparing a musical comedy. I'm hoping for the leading part." She stood and rocked on her heels.

He walked toward the door, but she cleared her throat. Turning back, he quirked an eyebrow.

"I hate to ask so early in our relationship, but I need money now. The rent on our rooms is due today."

He motioned for her to follow him across the hall to his study. Opening a drawer in his desk, he pulled out a lockbox and retrieved several notes, holding them out to her. "Will this do?"

Her cheeks flamed red, but she nodded, not meeting his eyes. When she didn't step forward to retrieve the money, he strode around the desk and approached her.

The smell of lilacs tickled his senses as he came closer. Her fingers brushed his as she took the notes, and his breath caught at the tingling sensation that ran up his arm.

Shaking his head and clasping his hands behind his back, he asked, "How is your father faring this morning?"

"Nothing a little hair of the dog won't fix. Or so he tells me." She still didn't look up, and the hairs on his neck pricked.

"Does he drink to excess often?"

Her flush extended up her face to the tips of her ears. "I'd prefer we not discuss my father."

Understanding what she was not saying, he nodded and led her from the room into the hall. He bit his cheek to keep from prying further but wondered if her father was a violent drunk. Was she safe around him?

He was her patron. He could not back out. But he might discern a way to make her father more presentable.

"If you need anything else, please contact me." Nodding, she moved toward the front door, but before her hand touched the knob he said, "I hope you get your desired part in the next production."

She rewarded him with a small smile. "Thank you again for your understanding. And for your patronage. Perhaps now I'll gain the notice of society, as Mrs. Siddon has done with her tragedies."

"The queen of comedy."

"Exactly." She dipped into a curtsy. "Good day, Your Grace."

"Good day to you, Miss Courteney."

Jonathan leaned back in his desk chair by the fire, rubbing his fingers over his lips. Outside, the wind rapped against the windowpanes, clamoring to be let in. The clouds hid the stars, no moonlight shining through. A damp smell hung in the air.

But none of his thoughts were focused on the weather. Instead of signing the paperwork to have a tenant's roof repaired or going over the harvest lists sitting on the desk in front of him, his mind would focus on only one thing.

Miss Courteney. He pictured her earlier that day, standing in this very room, wearing a mixture of emotions. He imagined needing his money was not an easy thing for her to admit. Yet she'd rallied enough courage to do so. And managed the thing without appearing weak or uncertain. He admired her strength of character.

Aside from supporting her financially, he wanted to be a useful patron. What could he do, within the bounds of propriety, of course, to help further her career? He knew little about the theatre community or how it worked. Beyond enjoying a performance whenever possible and reading the occasional review in the paper, he didn't busy himself with the nuances of that community.

Based on their previous conversation, giving his opinion on roles that would suit her did not seem like an option. Bribing the right people to get her leading roles might be frowned upon, but he was willing to spread some money around for her cause. But not knowing who to bribe meant that plan wouldn't work.

The door opened behind him, and Jonathan lifted his chair by the arms, turning in his seat to face his desk once more. His mother stood framed in the doorway, light from the hallway behind her shadowing her face.

"Rather late to be working." She strolled into the room, wrapping her arms around herself as her eyes darted to the portrait of Jonathan's father hanging over the mantel behind him, then looking away just as quickly.

"I'm not. Too distracted." He cleared his throat. "Perhaps you can help me. I've recently volunteered myself as a patron for a talented actress."

His mother arched an eyebrow.

"There is nothing wrong with my being a patron of the theatre."

"No, there is not. What is it you need help with?" She kept a straight face, but Jonathan wondered why his mother would think him a cad. Only a man with no respect for his mother would ask her for help with problems concerning his mistress.

"I am wondering what I can do to help her." Besides giving her a stipend to help support her, he thought but didn't say.

"Has she ever been interviewed for a biographical piece in any of the ladies' periodicals? *La Belle Assemblée* or perhaps *The Lady's Monthly Museum*?"

Sitting up in his chair, Jonathan shrugged, but his mind began churning. "I don't know, but probably not. Do you think they would interview her if I wrote them suggesting it?"

"You are a duke. I doubt they would refuse." Another glance at the portrait hanging behind him caught his attention.

"Are you missing him?" He stood and walked around his desk, putting his hands under her elbows.

"Oh, a little more than usual, I suppose. On blustery nights like these, I used to sneak into his room. I wasn't a very good sneak." A sparkle danced in her eyes. "He always knew I was there but pretended to be asleep so I could save face the next morning. I mean, who ever heard of an English woman who's scared of the rain?"

Pulling his mother into a hug, Jonathan chuckled. "No one, and no one ever shall. Why don't we ring for some tea and find you a novel? At least that way, if the storm keeps you up, you can pretend it is because you were reading a good book."

With a short sniff, she nodded. "That sounds perfect." Breaking away, she strode around the room, studying the books on the shelves while Jonathan arranged for tea to be sent up to her room.

Once she was settled, he took his own tea in the study and pulled out a fresh sheet of paper. He had a few letters to write before bed.

Chapter 5

I SI STOOD ON THE duke's doorstep once more, staring up at the intimidating stone building. He had summoned her for a meeting. The air still held a hint of chill, but the sun was quickly warming the world. Morning sunlight reflected off the white stone, blinding her. Blinking, she stepped forward into the shadow of the doorway and waited for someone to answer her knock. She had contemplated bringing Mary along as chaperone but wasn't ready to divulge her newfound patron to the rest of the troupe just yet.

Still, as she waited for the door to open, goosebumps rose on her arms. What if he had lied or changed his mind about not wanting favors from her? She couldn't simply return his money and walk away—she'd already used it to pay rent on their rooms. Aside from that, he was much larger than her, not looming like a giant, but with shoulders that filled his coat, she knew he could overpower her, regardless of her feelings on the matter.

Just as she turned to flee, the door opened, and the butler bowed in greeting, stepping back to allow her entry.

Filling her lungs with the smoggy town air, she forced her feet across the threshold and into the foyer.

"Just a moment." The butler strode over to the study door and knocked. A muffled voice bid him enter, and the man opened the door. "She is here, Your Grace."

"Wonderful, show her in."

The power in his voice reminded her to be on her guard. He couldn't demand she make an appearance at his every whim. And she would tell him so. That was not part of their agreement. Perhaps they needed to set things down on paper. Just because she was grateful for his financial assistance did not mean she would bend to his will.

As she moved into the room, she opened her mouth to speak but stopped when she saw they weren't alone. A lady sat in a spindly chair beside an empty matching chair while another man sat behind the duke's desk.

The duke himself stood with his hands behind his back next to the lady who, upon further inspection, held a writing box on her lap and a quill in her hand.

"Miss Courteney, wonderful of you to come." The duke stepped forward, a polite smile gracing his face. "May I introduce Mrs. Hughes and Mr. Ballinger. They are from *The Lady's Monthly Museum.*"

"Pleased to meet you." Isi nodded her head to them both before rounding her questioning gaze on him.

"Please forgive me for not rising, but my box is a bit cumbersome. Have a seat and we'll get started." Mrs. Hughes waved her hand at the empty chair beside her.

Tearing her eyes away from the duke, Isi sat on the edge of the seat, feeling as though she were perched atop a crumbling wall that might fall out from under her at any moment.

The woman glanced down at a few sheets of paper placed on her writing box.

"I'm sorry," Isi said after a silent moment, "what are we starting?"

"The interview, of course."

"Interview?"

"For a sketch of you. For the magazine."

"You're going to write an article on me for *The Lady's Monthly Museum?*" Isi felt her voice catch in her throat, and her eyes darted around the room again, stopping momentarily on the man sitting behind the desk. He stared at her, frowning, then looked down at a paper in front of him, sticking his tongue out and drawing something. Why was he frowning?

Shifting in her seat, she caught the duke's eye as he stood before a bookshelf, open book in his hands.

"Care to explain?" She fought to keep her voice steady. An interview in a popular woman's magazine could do wonders for her career, but could he not have mentioned this in the note he'd sent summoning her here? Wisps of hair escaped at the nape of her neck and her dress was a few seasons behind the current trends. She smoothed her hair, wishing for a mirror to help her tuck her wayward strands back in. While she loved an audience, an audience of one was a much more discerning crowd. And she wouldn't be playing a role but baring her life for others to read about. What would she say if they asked about her father?

"I just want to be helpful. Feel as though I'm contributing something to your career. Besides, what better way to introduce you to society than by telling them who you are?" He shrugged and closed the book, slipping it back on the shelf.

"And who is he?" she gestured with her head to the man whose name she'd forgotten.

But it was Mrs. Hughes who answered. "Mr. Ballinger will sketch a portrait of you for the engraving that will accompany the article."

Isi felt her eyes shoot up her forehead. Had she known that, she would have taken more care with her hair.

"Shall we get started?" Mrs. Hughes held her quill pen at the ready.

"I suppose." Isi sat up straight, shaking her shoulders back.

"Tell me about your troupe, your last performance, and what you are planning next."

Unsure what the woman was looking for, Isi clasped her hands in her lap and tried to appear more confident than she felt. "We last performed a romantic comedy where I played the part of abigail to Miss Mary Robinson's lady. The troupe leader is Mr. David Martin, and he has a particular gift for choosing plays with excellent ensemble parts that suit everyone."

"And how did you end up with Mr. Martin's troupe?"

"My mother and father were part of the troupe before I was born. Mr. Martin is like an uncle to me."

"How long have you been performing?" The scratch of the quill flying across the paper as Mrs. Hughes wrote down her answers meant the woman wasn't looking at her much.

Mr. Ballinger, on the other hand, hardly took his eyes off of her. His black and grey hair combed, back away from his face, made his cheeks look larger, and his tendency to stick out his tongue as he drew gave him an almost frog-like appearance—or that of a squirrel with nuts in its cheeks.

"Since I was a young girl, maybe twelve, although I may have played other roles when I was very small." Behind her, she heard the duke slide another book off the shelf before he moved into her line of sight, taking up position on a cushioned stool near the door.

He stuck his legs out in front of him and looked more like a young boy sitting on the shorter piece of furniture, his shoulders slouching against the wall. If any of his peers could see him now, they wouldn't recognize him as a duke. Somehow, he looked more human. More like anyone else Isi might associate with.

His relaxed manner set her at ease until Mrs. Hughes asked her next question.

"You said your parents are part of the troupe as well?"

"My father is. He works behind the scenes. My mother was an actress before she passed away. Mrs. Courteney." Isi bit her lip and wondered if the woman would know of her mother.

But Mrs. Hughes barely glanced up from her papers. "I'm sorry for your loss. How long ago did she pass?"

"Four years ago." Isi could barely force the words out in a whisper.

The scratching of the quill continued, and Isi's blood began to pound in her ears. Her mother would be reduced to a detail in this article. A passing comment included only because of her connection to Isi. She had been a talented actress and deserved better. Isi didn't even deserve this interview. She hadn't earned it by performing well, the way Mrs. Siddons had. She hadn't even had a leading role yet. What a fraud she was!

"And what is next for your troupe?" Mrs. Hughes moved on.

Isi swallowed the lump in her throat. Deserved or not, this would be good publicity for the troupe, and perhaps Mr. Martin might give her a more robust part in the next production. She could finally begin living up to her mother's legacy. "We're preparing a musical comedy. I'm not sure I can tell you the name as we've only just begun, and parts haven't yet been assigned. I can say it promises to be a lot of fun."

"And what other interests do you have?"

Isi did not make a habit of reading many magazines. They were a luxury she couldn't afford, but she wondered if the questions were the same every time. The article, though a sketch of her and her life, would hardly be personal. A few details describing her life and history did not give the full picture of who she was, even if they included an engraving of her. This would be just another version of her, another facade. Would no one ever see her for the hard working, dedicated actress she was?

Her gaze rested on the duke, who still sat staring at his book, though he hadn't turned a page yet. Was he listening to her answers? Why had he arranged this interview? He was a busy, important man who hardly needed to concern himself with an actress who hadn't even held a leading role.

"Um, I don't have many interests. Outside of rehearsals, I suppose I enjoy a nice gathering of friends; card games or a dance are welcome diversions. But mostly I spend time at the theatre or running lines on my own."

Another lengthy silence as the Mrs. Hughes scrawled notes on her papers gave Isi time to study the duke. His wavy brown hair curled around his ears and at the nape of his neck. The gentle slope of his shoulders belied the power she suspected he hid beneath his well-tailored coats. Did he practice with Gentleman Jackson?

He had never treated her as beneath him, even the night they'd met. In fact, recalling their conversation backstage that evening, she realized he had never said or even implied in a look anything improper. She had jumped to conclusions and rushed to defend her honor. No one else would do it for her, she knew, especially with her father in the state he'd been in.

Still perhaps she'd been hasty in jumping to such a conclusion. He'd given her no reason to believe him anything other than honorable. After she'd slapped him, he had every right to have her thrown in prison—striking a peer of the realm was illegal, after all. But he hadn't. His blush when she'd accused him of wanting to take her as his mistress could have been embarrassment at her shouting such things at him rather than a sign of guilt that that was his intention.

Nor had he asked anything of her when she'd later come to him all but begging him to become her patron and provide her with the money she needed for rent. And now with this interview, could he really just be interested in helping her further her career? He'd asked for nothing and would not benefit from the publication of the article.

Could he simply be a good man who saw some talent in her?

"I think that is all we need. How much longer do you require, Mr. Ballinger?" Mrs. Hughes tapped her papers together and opened her writing box, sliding the papers and quill inside before shutting the lid.

"Another ten minutes or so." The man's eyes darted up to study Isi again before returning to the paper in front of him.

"Shall I ring for tea?" The duke asked, rising fluidly from the stool.

"No, we won't keep you. You must be a busy man. We'll just let Mr. Ballinger finish up and get out of your way."

He nodded, his hands twisting his book around.

"Would you like to stay for tea, Miss Courteney?"

"I can't. I actually came from the theatre and need to return." A small pang of regret hummed in her chest, but she took a deep breath to steady herself again. "But thank you for offering. Perhaps another time."

"Yes. Perhaps we might find time for a game of cards then." A small smile on his face answered her earlier question about whether he'd been listening to the interview.

"I look forward to it. A rousing game of casino is one of my favorite things."

This conversation was much more personal than the interview, and Isi found herself sincerely hoping she might have the chance to play cards with the duke.

A short time later, Mr. Ballinger stood, and the duke saw them all out.

Leaving the man's townhome, Isi wondered again if she misjudged the duke. Maybe he truly did not want anything from her. Maybe he just enjoyed the theatre and wanted to see more of her on the stage. A warmth in her chest that had nothing to do with the late morning sun carried her all the way back to the theatre.

Chapter 6

JONATHAN HAD TAKEN NO more than two steps back toward his study when a knock sounded at the door. Had Miss Courteney changed her mind about tea? Tugging on the bottom of his coat, he turned and waited for the butler to open the door. His lips turned down in a frown when he saw the two ladies standing on the doorstep.

Mrs. and Miss Gibbon curtsied.

"How good to see you again, Your Grace," Mrs. Gibbon said as they entered.

Shaking his head to clear his thoughts, Jonathan nodded. "You as well. Are you here to see Mother?"

"We are, but of course you must stay and visit with us as well." Miss Gibbon tilted her head, smiling up at him and batting her lashes.

"I'm afraid I can only stay until Mother arrives to entertain you. I have things to attend to." It wasn't a lie. A stack of papers on his desk waited for him, but now he would gather his things and escape to his solicitor's office. Staying home was not an option.

Just then a footman descended the stairs. "Her grace will be down momentarily."

Jonathan waved his hand in the direction of the open door to the parlor and followed the ladies inside, his feet protesting the whole way.

"Who was that young lady we saw leaving just as we arrived? She looked familiar, but I couldn't place her." Mrs. Gibbon sat back on the couch with a sigh, then stared at him, waiting for an answer to her question, her owl-like eyes unnerving him. Miss Gibbon perched beside her mother and gave him an almost identical look.

He cleared his throat and tugged at the knot in his cravat. "That was Miss Courteney. We saw her when we last visited the theatre." He sat in a chair across from the couch and crossed his legs.

Miss Gibbon scrunched her brow, then her eyes widened. "The actress who played the maid?"

"Yes. I had arranged—well Mother helped arrange—an interview for her in *The Lady's Monthly Museum.*"

She shook her head as though in disbelief. "Why would you arrange all of that for an actress? One that didn't even have a lead role?" Her cheeks were red when she looked up at him again, as though her thoughts had taken her to the same place as Miss Courteney's had when he'd offered to be her patron.

Mrs. Gibbon sat up straighter now, eyeing him suspiciously, her lips pursed.

"I've offered to be her patron. I want to help her career as I believe she has talent. That is all." He tried to keep his voice firm, hoping that would close the matter.

Miss Gibbon opened her mouth but before she could speak, Mother walked in.

"Good day, ladies." She nodded at the two women and walked over to stand beside Jonathan's chair. He rose, adjusting his coat sleeves and tugging his waistcoat down.

"Have you rung for tea?" she asked.

He shook his head, and she nodded. "Might I offer you some tea?"

"Please." Mrs. Gibbon was nothing but pleasant now, her expression smoothed over.

Miss Gibbon, however, still sat perched on the edge of her seat with a frown on her face.

Mother rang the bell then moved back toward Jonathan, who scooted out of her way, gesturing for her to take his seat.

"If you ladies will excuse me." Jonathan made to leave the room.

"Wait, please, Your Grace. I've just had a wonderful idea." Miss Gibbon voice was a touch more shrill than normal. Whatever her idea was, Jonathan doubted he would describe it as *wonderful.*

He turned back and raised his eyebrows questioningly.

"You say you wish to help this young lady's career? You should host a party, introduce her to society properly."

Jonathan didn't pause for a moment. "No." He glanced at his mother who met his gaze with her steady one. She inclined her head just slightly toward Miss Gibbon as though he should consider her idea.

"Allow society to get to know her outside of those small roles she plays."

He held back a wince at her slight toward Miss Courteney. It was true, she hadn't yet held a leading role.

"Not to overstep, but as it was my idea, I would be happy to assist in planning the party." Miss Gibbon turned her attention to Mother, and Jonathan did the same.

Mother studied him from head to toe. He knew she saw his discomfort despite the way he relaxed his shoulders, trying to hide the tension building in him. Parties meant crowds, people he would be expected to talk to. It was bad enough attending such events, let alone hosting them, which he did as little as he could.

It wasn't fair to Mother the way he always reluctantly agreed when she asked if they could host an evening during the season. And Miss Gibbon was right. Exposing Miss Courteney to society could help her position in her theatre troupe.

The thought of an evening spent among his peers and their wives gave him a headache, but it would also give him a chance to see Miss Courteney again, in a proper setting.

He sighed, and his mother smiled at Miss Gibbon. "I would be pleased to have you help plan the party. Let me get a pen and we can start right away."

"When will this event take place?" Jonathan asked, his hand hovering on the parlor doorknob as he watched his mother move to the writing desk near the window.

"How does Friday sound?" she asked as she gathered a quill and some paper.

"Sounds fine." Jonathan nodded to the Gibbons and made his retreat to his study, shutting the door firmly behind him.

He sat behind the desk and rifled through the piles of papers on top. But his eyes wouldn't focus, the words blurring before him. Tapping the papers together he set them back down and pushed out of the chair. Clasping his hands behind his back, he paced on the other side of the desk, glancing up at his father's portrait every now and then.

When his Father couldn't hear himself think, he would usually go for a ride. Not wanting to wait for a horse to be readied, Jonathan opted for a walk instead. Poking his head out of the door of the study, he listened to the women's voices coming from the parlor. He felt like a schoolboy ditching class as he tiptoed down the hall to the front door and slipped outside.

Warmth from the sun's rays kept the brisk spring breeze from chilling him. Instead he found the cool air refreshing. He hoped it might help clear his thoughts.

He hosted only a few events each season, and only for the sake of his mother. She enjoyed hostessing, and she had a talent for creating enjoyable evenings no matter who they were entertaining.

Enjoyable for some people, anyway.

For Jonathan, each event felt like a test. Did he live up to the expectations society placed upon him? Was he showing off his wealth enough, but not overly flaunting it as though he were trying too hard? Did he make enough important decisions to be an influence in parliament? Were his affairs in order? His estates maintained?

On top of all that, every mother wanted a duke for her daughter. He avoided parties and other social gatherings not only because large groups gave him hives, but because he'd nearly been trapped alone in a room with a woman intent on becoming a duchess on multiple occasions, only just escaping before damage was done to either of their reputations.

He glanced up from the cobblestones surprised to find he'd nearly walked all the way to the Drury Lane Theatre. His breathing was labored, and he must have been walking faster than he'd realized. In the back of his mind, he wondered if this had always been his destination. Even as he told himself he should turn around and go home, he wandered further into the shadow of the building.

He pulled on the door, pleased at how little resistance it gave, and entered the lobby. The lush carpets and papered walls were dim with light coming in the windows, dust motes swirling through the air.

Noise floated to him from the auditorium. He made his way toward his box.

"Excuse me, sir, you can't be here," a voice said from his right.

Turning, he watched a man hurry across the lobby from the direction of the ticket windows. The man adjusted his coat. "I'm sorry. Rehearsals are taking place. I encourage you to come back tonight for a show or—"

"Would it help if I told you I'm the Duke of Edston and wish to sit in my box, for which I pay handsomely, and view rehearsals?"

The man slowly shook his head but glanced behind him as though to be sure they weren't being watched.

Jonathan pulled out several notes, holding them out to the young man, who licked his lips, his eyes widening. Scratching the back of his neck, he reached out with his other hand and took the notes.

With a nod, he shoved them in his pocket and said, "Very good, sir. I never saw you, if anyone asks."

"Might I ask one more thing?" Jonathan removed one more note. "A piece of paper, pen, and ink."

Once the man had retrieved the items from the desks behind the ticket counters, Jonathan made his way to his box and quietly sidled inside, sitting near enough to the edge to see the stage, but far enough back to be inconspicuous in the shadows.

Below, the troupe were sitting around the stage on crates, armchairs, spindly slat-back chairs, anything they could find, it seemed—some even sat on the floor, dangling their legs off the edge of the platform.

In the center one man stood, surveying everyone and speaking about parts for their upcoming production.

Jonathan quickly located Miss Courteney, her auburn hair shimmering even in the dim lighting. Was there any lighting in which she didn't shine?

Several stage hands, including Mr. Courteney, ambled around checking ropes for frayed ends and moving large props, readying for the performance that night. The man didn't sway or veer around as he walked, which boded well. He couldn't say for certain, but the man didn't appear to be drunk.

As the meeting continued, he began writing a note to Miss Courteney. Though he would have liked to extend the invitation to the party in person, he did not want to intrude on rehearsals more than he already was. He also hoped a note would feel less personal and intimidating than an invitation issued personally by a duke. Perhaps her hackles wouldn't be raised so much at the less personal written invitation, as he did not wish to raise her suspicions that he wanted more.

Which was ridiculous since his station in life, society's expectations of him, and his reputation—more importantly, her reputation—made any further relationship between them impossible.

The distorted echoing voice of the troupe leader carried to Jonathan's box, but he couldn't understand the words. He noticed Miss Courteney's shoulders slump for a moment before she rallied, sitting taller, head held high.

How did she do that—keep her chin up when something hadn't gone her way?

When Miss Gibbon last visited Mother, the girl had complained about missing a ball because her parents had already accepted an invitation to a dinner party. The topic of her disappointment had come about because Mother had complimented the silky forest green shawl Miss Gibbon had bought to console herself.

Yet when something went amiss in Miss Courteney's life, she simply shook herself out of the doldrums and moved on.

Was it because her ultimate goal was a personal one? Something she valued as worth the fight? Becoming a darling of the stage and captivating audiences was a matter of hard work on her part and catching the attention of the *ton*, which he was trying to facilitate as best he could. But ultimately, her drive to achieve her dream was unique.

Miss Gibbon had no goal for herself beyond marrying well, which many young women did each season with hardly any effort. Indeed, if their parents arranged an advantageous marriage for them, no work was required at all.

What was he working toward? He kept busy between the responsibilities of maintaining his estates, his parliamentary duties, and the social events his mother lined up for them during the season. But none of that fulfilled him the way performing seemed to fulfill Miss Courteney.

A longing ache deepened in his chest. Tearing his eyes away from the scene below, he finished his note and signed it, then left in search of the man he'd paid off before to gain access to his box.

In the lobby near the ticket counters, a young boy dawdled about with a wooden top.

"Boy, are you familiar with the actors of theatre company that is rehearsing here today?" Jonathan strode over to the lad, swinging his arms, the note folded in his hand.

The young man nodded, his eyes widening slightly as he tilted his head back to look up at Jonathan.

"Can you deliver this note to Miss Courteney?"

The child scratched his chin and slapped a hand down on his wobbling top. He eyed the note and then Jonathan again, who reached for his purse and pulled out a coin, holding it up. "One now, and one when you return to confirm she received the note."

Snatching the coin from his hand, the boy straightened and reached for the note, then took off into the depths of the theatre.

He contemplated returning to his box to be sure the boy discharged his duty but knew he would have a difficult time leaving the theatre if he laid eyes on Miss Courteney once again. She had a captivating way about her.

Feeling optimistic, he stared out the window. Despite having to host a party, he found himself looking forward to an event that was not attending the theatre, for once. A party at which it would be acceptable for him to visit with Miss Courteney and discover more about her.

Chapter 7

Isi blew stray strands of hair out of her face and held in a sigh. David had just assigned parts for the musical comedy, and though she had a part, it was not the one she'd wanted. Standing, she made her way across the stage toward David to discuss her disappointment, but he became engaged in a conversation about sets, so she looked over her lines and waited for an opportunity to get his attention.

Flipping through the script, her thoughts turned to the Duke, as they often had for the past few days. He had offered to help get her the part she wanted. But could she damage her career by forcing herself into an unsuitable role if David didn't think she was ready for a lead?

She wanted audiences to love her, to come to her shows because she was in them, because watching her brought them joy.

Her troupe's productions always brought in money and ran longer than many other plays. However, the audience felt flat, more two dimensional than the characters she portrayed. They came for different purposes than she wanted in an ideal audience. They were the spectacle. People attended to visit, size each other up, and flaunt their wealth.

As she sat on a large crate, a small boy approached with a note. "This just came for you, Miss Courteney."

She tousled his hair with a smile and reached for the paper, but the boy pulled it back and held out his hand, attempting to hide an impish grin.

"Of course. One moment." She stood and pulled a coin out of her purse, handing it to him, wishing she didn't have to tally up how much money she had left and how much she needed to get her and her father through the week.

With a nod of his cap, the boy handed her the note and ran off amongst the props and costumes backstage.

She unfolded the paper wondering who would send her a note via messenger. Her eyes dropped to the signature. Why would his grace be writing to her?

Dear Miss Courteney,

At the urging of a friend, I have arranged for a soirée this Friday evening. It seems my friend believes that introducing you to the ton *might help you. Perhaps if your name is bandied about amongst society, it will influence Mr. Martin to give you more central roles. As the guest list is filled with stuffy gentlemen and their wives along with any young people who are out in society, it promises to be a dull evening. At least when compared to attending a theatre performance with the Queen of Comedy. I would, therefore, like to extend an invitation to you, in the hopes that you will lighten things up. Perhaps we might play a game of casino or whist. Will you do me the honor?*

Sincerely,

J. Sterling, Duke of Edston

"What have you got there?" her father asked over her shoulder.

She shielded the note from him. "Oh, just an invitation to a party." She examined him, wondering when he'd last had a drink.

His eyes were the clearest she'd seen in weeks, and he hadn't slurred his words. He stood there without swaying, and she allowed herself a small smile.

"Are you going?" He pointed at the note. "When is it?"

"At the end of the week. I think I might. Once the show starts, we won't have any more free nights." She held up her script.

"I heard. That's a good part. I'm sure it's leading to bigger things. Soon." He gave her shoulder a squeeze, and her breath caught. Warmth seeped along her limbs. Papa hadn't been sober in months.

"What did you do last night?"

He grinned. "I slept. Fell asleep at the tavern yesterday morning and didn't wake until this morning."

"You slept the whole day and night?"

He nodded and puffed his chest out.

That explained it. But she couldn't knock him unconscious any time he overindulged.

David walked over and put his arm around her father's shoulders. "I need to speak with you." He led her father away, and she watched them go, neither one of them glancing back at her.

Fingering the note in her hand, her heart fluttered faster at the thought of seeing the Duke. He'd even remembered that she enjoyed playing cards. And maybe if she met more of the people who attended their performances, the audience might not feel so flat to her. With a glance about the room, she found a scrap of paper and scrawled a hasty note accepting the invitation. Then she tracked down the scamp who had delivered the note and after bribing him with another coin convinced him to carry her reply back to his grace.

Stuffing the note in her reticule, Isi gripped her script in one hand and marched over to David and her father, who stood discussing the timing of their next production and whether her father would need the help of another to pull all the ropes.

As she approached, David's attention flicked to her.

With a deep breath, she opened her mouth to speak. But her father did so first.

"We are so grateful to you David." He wrapped his arm around Isi's shoulders with a squeeze and a smile. "The part you gave Isi is perfect for her. I'm sure it will help fill out her experience."

Biting her lips together to keep from saying anything, Isi nodded. She had been acting on stage for half of her life now. But more experience never hurt, she supposed.

"I'm always glad to have her in productions. She's so like her mother." David's eyes stayed on her as though looking for the similarities. Though Isi felt the compliment deeply, having seen her mother perform her entire life, she wished for more of her mother's spirit. She couldn't imagine her mother settling for a smaller part if she felt she could act better a different role.

After a moment, David clapped her father on the shoulder and walked away. Turning, she noticed tears brimming in her father's eyes before he coughed to clear his throat. "Excuse me, I'll just—" He made toward the back exit of the building and Isi had the sinking feeling he wouldn't be sober for long.

Arriving at the Duke's spacious townhouse, Isi's stomach rolled, and she felt a mixture of nausea and dizziness.

"Are you well?" Mary asked, noting how Isi clutched her friend's arm tighter.

In the dim light of night with only small dim circles cast by streetlights and the glow of candlelight from the windows shining from the imposing stone facade, Isi questioned everything about her decision to attend the Duke's soiree.

Her dress, borrowed from the theatre's collection of costumes, swished just above her toes. If she wasn't careful, she might trip on it. Grasping her silk wrap tighter around her shoulders, she was grateful for what little warmth it provided. Though the day had been nice, the nights were still cold early in March.

Asking Mary to chaperone her made her almost as nervous. What if the duke or his guests were unkind toward Mary? She knew her friend wouldn't let any rude comments get to her. She'd grown thick skin from years of being an actress and having people judge and criticize her performances. But there was no reason for Mary to be there tonight besides the fact that she was a good friend and mentor to Isi.

Mary coughed behind her gloved hand.

"I'm fine. But if you're feeling poorly, we can leave." Isi turned, ready to flee the front steps.

But Mary held her in place, patting her hand. "It's nothing. A tickle in my throat."

Steeling herself, Isi straightened and nodded, keeping her eyes trained forward as they entered.

The duke, his mother, and another young woman stood in the foyer, greeting the guests as they arrived. He and his mother looked enough alike that no one could mistake them for anything other than family. They had the same wavy brown hair and honey-colored eyes that warmed when they smiled.

The duke looked down the line of people until his eyes stopped on Isi, and a smile softened the lines puckering around his eyes. A fluttering in her stomach replaced the nausea she'd felt just outside.

When he turned his attention back to the guest in front of him, Isi examined the rich dark wood trim of the hall. Each piece of furniture, every decoration on the walls, was perfectly suited to the space. A few small portraits hung nearby, giving the place a homey feel, while against another wall, a simple table held a vase overflowing with lilacs and pale yellow hollyhocks.

As the line moved forward, Isi watched the duke. He wore a deep blue coat cut to his figure, a cream waistcoat, and beige breeches. Though his eyes continued to dart down the line to her, he didn't smile as wide as when he'd first spied her. As another couple moved away from the hosts, he reached up to rub at the back of his neck for a moment before shaking the sleeves of his jacket down his arm to straighten them, his fingers fidgeting with the hem of his waistcoat and the cuffs of his shirt.

He seemed as uncomfortable as she'd felt just outside.

She watched him greet a few more people before it was their turn, and with each interaction, she became more certain that he was not enjoying himself. Curtsying, she bobbed her head low. "Your grace. Thank you for the invitation this evening."

"The pleasure is mine." She felt more than saw his eyes upon her, taking in her figure, and held her breath for a moment until their eyes met once more. The fire she saw in them told her far more than he could ever say in present company and she exhaled, glad he approved of her borrowed dress. The sky-blue slip hugged her figure, teasing the viewer beneath a white crepe overlay. She'd felt quite fetching in it before leaving the theatre with Mary earlier in the evening.

"Mother, may I present Miss Courteney. Miss Courteney, my mother the Duchess of Edston."

His mother studied her, and though her eyes were the same color as her sons, the warmth she'd seen in his gaze did not reside in hers. She did not seem cold, simply contemplative as she studied Isi.

Next to the duke, a young lady cleared her throat.

Blinking, his grace held out a hand. "Forgive me. Miss Gibbon, Miss Courteney."

Miss Gibbon held the duke's hand as she dipped into a curtsy. "I've heard so much about you from his grace. When he told me he'd sponsored you, I insisted he have a party so his friends could meet you."

Isi held her smile in place and noticed that Miss Gibbon did not remove her hand from the duke's right away. "How delightful. I enjoy a good party. This is my good friend, Mrs. Mary Reynolds." The group nodded in acknowledgement as Mary curtsied.

"Mother, if you'll excuse me, I'll escort Miss Courteney and Mrs. Reynolds around and introduce them to my friends, as Miss Gibbon suggested." Isi could see the tension leaving his shoulders as he stepped slightly out of line.

"You'll do no such thing. Guests are still arriving and you are the host." Her words would have seemed harsh had they not been spoken with tender affection. She placed a hand on her son's arm, comforting him.

The duke's eyes glazed over, and he stepped back beside his mother.

"I would be delighted to introduce Miss Courteney around." Miss Gibbon took a step forward, looping her hand through Isi's arm. Though her tone was warm, her smile was stiff as the duchess excused them.

Miss Gibbon shuffled Isi along and Mary followed behind, trying to keep up with their weaving in and out of small groups of people. She coughed again, and Isi glanced back, wondering if her friend really was well. Her cheeks were flushed, but that could be a result of coming into the warm house from the cold.

Isi wondered if Miss Gibbon meant to introduce them to anyone as she passed through the hall and rooms so quickly, her grip on Isi's arm never lessening. Perhaps the girl meant to parade her around and then abandon her to the mercy of the *ton*.

But as they entered a room at the end of the hall, she slowed her steps and nodded toward a small grouping of young ladies standing near the fireplace, drinking punch.

"Ladies, you must meet Miss Courteney. She is an actress at Drury Lane and His Grace has, graciously, become her patron." She wrinkled her nose at her play on words, and the girls giggled.

"Miss Courteney, this is Miss Bauer, Miss Terry, Miss Warner, and Miss Potter. This is Miss Courteney and her friend, Mrs. Reynolds, also an actress." Miss Gibbon dropped Isi's arm and stood beside the other girls, who studied Isi and Mary as one might study an exotic animal at the Royal Menagerie.

"I do believe I saw your last show," Miss Bauer said. "The man in your last production, the one pretending to be a duke, was not as handsome as I thought he should have been."

"Why would that matter?" asked Miss Terry, who stood nearest the fireplace. Her skin glowed in the firelight, though Isi wondered how she was not roasting so near the heat.

"If he were really a duke, it wouldn't. He could be old and fat, and I'd still marry him," said another girl in a pink dress whose name Isi couldn't remember.

"Most of them are, but I doubt he'd have you," said Miss Gibbon beside Miss Bauer.

The girl in the pink dress turned up her nose and walked away. Mary stepped back to allow the girl to pass.

"But you're right, Miss Bauer. It is much more pleasant watching a romance when the two people falling in love are pleasing to the eye. Don't you agree, Miss Courteney?" Miss Gibbon eyed her, glancing up and down, studying Isi's dress.

Tugging on the white crepe fabric of her dress, Isi wished she were better with a needle. Had she any experience in needlework, she might have added a few tucks to the dress to accentuate her figure more and lifted the hem just enough that she wouldn't need to be mindful not to step on it. "Indeed, though it would hardly be an accurate portrayal of life."

"And the theatre is always accurate." The girls giggled, and Miss Gibbon went on. "You're right though. I always feel terrible when I hear of a couple marrying when one of them is unequal to the other, especially in looks, but it happens more often than not."

"Surely physical appearance is not the most important thing to consider when making a match," said one girl. The cut of her dress did not flatter her curvier body and Isi felt sorry that the current fashion trends didn't lend themselves to such a figure.

"Certainly not. A kind rotund husband would be preferable to a handsome drunk," said Isi.

"Quite right. The way a man treats his wife is more important than whether his nose is slightly crooked or his ears are a bit large." Mary smiled warmly at the girl.

Miss Gibbon pursed her lips looking up at the ceiling. "Perhaps. It would depend on one's motives for marrying."

Isi narrowed her eyes. "What are your motives?"

The group fell into silence glancing between Isi and Miss Gibbon. Miss Gibbon smiled, but her eyes blazed.

"I wasn't speaking specifically. Just generally." She waved her hand about the group. "Some girls are looking for a man in his dotage, hoping to be rich widows. Others for money to save their family from ruin, and others obsess over a title."

"And which category do you fit in?" Isi pressed.

Miss Gibbon sidestepped the question. "Whomever I marry, I do hope to find a man my equal in looks. It will be so satisfying to parade about, drawing everyone's attention."

Isi looked her up and down and smiled. "Well, the man you marry will have a lot to live up to." She was pleased at the brief confusion that flashed across Miss Gibbon's face.

She recovered, jutting her chin up. "How sweet, thank you. But of course, I don't always look this beautiful. You should see me in the morning."

"I'm sure the duke and you will make a satisfactory match," said Miss Terry, putting her hand on Miss Gibbon's arm.

Miss Gibbon giggled and hid her mouth behind her hand, but her eyes flicked to Isi.

That's when she realized why Miss Gibbon had arranged this party. She thought Isi might be competition.

"What about you, Miss Courteney? What are your motives?"

"I have none." Isi shrugged. "Aside from performing as a darling of the stage."

The other girls assured her she was a delight to watch and lavished Mary with praise. They all promised to attend their next performance, but Miss Gibbon kept studying Isi, her eyes cold.

Chapter 8

J ONATHAN WATCHED FROM ACROSS the room as Miss Courteney stared down Miss Gibbon, whose smile had turned frosty. What were they discussing?

Miss Courteney gave Miss Gibbon a small, confident smile and curtsied, excusing herself from the group of young ladies. Her companion, Mrs. Reynolds followed her lead and they moved toward the door of the parlor. Not a few steps from the doorway, Mrs. Reynolds was stopped by Mrs. Lawring, and the two embraced, their smiles stretching with happiness.

Miss Courteney stopped for a moment, and Mrs. Reynolds introduced her to Mrs. Lawring. After a few minutes, she curtsied and began moving toward the door once again.

"You're staring. It's unseemly." Mother's voice floated up beside him.

Turning, he met her gaze with a steady one of his own. "I'm just assuring myself she isn't being mistreated."

"You're oddly protective of her. Should I be worried?" She pursed her lips and eyed him.

"Not at all. Of course I'm protective. I've invested in her future as an actress. It would be strange if I didn't worry about how that investment might play out." He turned away from his mother, clasping his hands behind his back and eyeing the door Miss Courteney had just gone through. "Her reputation can make or break her career, and you know better than I how important this party will be in gaining her the favor of the *ton*."

"Just be circumspect in your actions toward her this evening, and nothing will go amiss." With that, she glided away from him, across the room toward her group of friends.

Jonathan eyed the room once more, noting that Mrs. Reynolds was still visiting with Mrs. Lawring. The two must be old friends in need of catching up. But that left Miss Courteney alone among society. Though she'd handled Miss Gibbon with grace, he worried she might find some of the other guests to be less veiled in their view of her social station.

Swiftly, he left the room in search of her. He had checked the dining room, the drawing room, which they'd set up for dancing, and not finding her in either place, moved toward the music room, where tables had been set up for cards.

His pulse slowed as he saw her standing near a table, drinking a cup of punch, watching two of Miss Gibbon's friends playing casino. Edging around the room, he drew up beside her. "Miss Courteney."

"I wondered if I'd be seeing you at all this evening." She smirked and took another sip from her cup.

Ironic that he'd been watching her all evening, yet she'd failed to notice him. "I've been engaged with my many guests. I hope you haven't hurt for company."

"Not at all. I've been introduced to so many people, I'll never remember all of their names or faces." She tapped her fingers on the side of her empty glass. "But hopefully, they'll all remember me."

He chuckled. "I'm certain they will. Allow me." Reaching for her cup, his fingers brushed her gloved hands, and a tingle shot up his arm, causing him to fumble the glass.

Miss Courteney juggled her hands around his, until they were both supporting the cup. Then slowly, she pulled her fingers back, making sure he wasn't going to drop the glass again.

Turning, he set the glass down on a small cabinet against the wall behind him. He turned back to her, clearing his throat.

"Would you like to play a game?" He motioned to the table in front of them as the man and woman stood to leave.

"I do enjoy a good game." He pulled out the chair for her, noticing the twinkle in her eye.

"As do I. Though preferably with fewer people around to watch me fail." He sat back, glancing at the others in the room. Reaching for the deck of cards in the middle of the table, he began shuffling.

"I get the feeling you prefer to have fewer people around in general."

He nodded, expelling a chuckle with a breath.

She leaned forward across the table and lowered her voice. "Why host a party if you don't enjoy it?"

Tapping the cards together on the table, he began dealing out for a game of casino. "Regrettably, I do a great many things I don't enjoy. In the name of duty, mostly."

"Such as participating in Lords?"

"Among other things." He noticed Miss Gibbon enter the room with his mother, both of them speaking behind gloved hands. The pressure to marry someone appropriate and produce an heir came to mind as another thing he'd rather not deal with.

Miss Courteney picked up her cards and fanned them out, but her gaze pierced him instead of focusing on her hand. "Hosting this party is not one of your duties. Why do it?"

He cleared his throat and rearranged his hand. "On the contrary, when I became your patron, I took on some responsibility for your career. And since you won't allow me an opinion on which parts are right for you"—he paused, glancing up to see her smirking—"I must look for other ways to be of assistance."

Tapping her finger on the edge of her cards, she plucked one from her hand and placed it in the middle of the table. "I'm sorry to have added to your duties. It is a shame when the responsibilities thrust upon us are heavy to bear."

He noted the way her smile softened and her green eyes dulled. He felt the urge to reach across the table and offer her comfort, to ask about what burdens she carried, but out of the corner of his eye, he saw his mother and Miss Gibbon making their way around the edges of the room. So instead, he straightened and placed his own card on the table.

"Sometimes I wish my father were here so I could ask his advice." The words left his lips before he could think them through. He almost never spoke of his father, of how inadequate he felt playing the role of Duke of Edston.

But the shimmer in Miss Courteney's eyes and the way her smile quirked up on one side made the admission worth it.

"I feel the same. If my mother were here...there's so much I wish I had paid more attention to. So much she could have taught me." With a shrug, she swiped at her eyes and pulled another card from her hand.

"Exactly. And not just in dealing with estate matters or voting in Lords. I'd love to have his opinion on other topics as well, such as marriage." He felt heat creeping up his neck at that admission, so he quickly added, "Or whether or not to buy a horse."

Miss Courteney lowered her gaze, but not before he caught her biting her lips together to hold in her amusement.

Grinning, he placed his last card on the table. "Looks like you take this hand."

"Perhaps you should have sought council from your father on how to play cards."

"My husband was a terrible card player. However, if my son wishes for a tutor, I'm sure I could teach him a thing or two." Mother approached the table with a smile. Despite knowing her opinion on how close Jonathan should get to Miss Courteney, she showed no malice toward the girl. The same could not be said for Miss Gibbon. Her eyes were ice, and she crossed her arms over her chest, jutting her hip out.

"Perhaps we might play a game some time. I enjoy a challenge." Miss Courteney met Mother's gaze with her own.

Miss Gibbon snorted, then hid her mouth behind her hand as they all turned to her.

"I'm not certain when we shall be seeing one another again, but if we find ourselves in company with nothing better to do, I would enjoy a game or two."

Jonathan gathered the cards and began shuffling the deck. "Actually, that is something I am wondering also. Do you suppose, Miss

Courteney, you might find time in your busy schedule to go for a drive in Hyde Park with me?"

He didn't know why he felt the need to defend Miss Courteney. She'd handled Mother with grace, charm, and wit.

She understood him in a way his Mother and Miss Gibbon did not.

"I would be honored. I believe I am free tomorrow." She took the newly shuffled deck from his hands and began dealing out the next round.

With a huff, Miss Gibbon turned on her heel and stalked out of the room. His mother inclined her head at them both before making her way from the room in a more graceful manner.

"You'll be hearing their opinions on the matter of us driving out together later, I'd wager." Miss Courteney placed the deck on the table and picked up her cards.

"That's a bet you'd be collecting on." Jonathan picked up his own cards and hid his pleased smile behind them. Miss Gibbon and Mother could think what they would. He would be seeing Miss Courteney again the very next day. The thought of spending more time with her without having to host a party or find another excuse made his heart warm with pleasure.

The next day, Jonathan drove his phaeton from his townhome to Drury Lane. The morning mist was slow burning off, and it wasn't exactly the fashionable hour for a drive in the park, but Miss Courteney had rehearsals and a show to perform later. The clip-clop of the horses' hooves stopped in front of the theatre. Turning his head, he searched for someone to watch the horses. Before he found someone, the door opened, and Miss Courteney bounded out with a grin.

No other young lady had her exuberance. He couldn't help grinning as he descended the rig with an extra bounce in his step.

When she reached him, she placed a hand on her chest and caught his eye, her cheeks pinked. She straightened, lowering her hand to her side while trying to catch her breath without being obvious.

He held out his hand and waited, inhaling the scent of lilacs that tickled his nose.

She let out a final huff and pulled in a deep lungful of air before placing her gloved hand in his. Her dainty fingers belied the strength he noted sparkling in her green eyes.

He handed her up onto the seat and then walked around and climbed in beside her. They rode in silence as he ushered the horses on toward Hyde Park.

"The party last night seemed a success."

"Yes, I believe it pleased Miss Gibbon." He cleared his throat, wondering why it was so hard to talk to her today.

Miss Courteney chuckled. "I can hardly believe that."

"It was well attended, and the arrangements she'd helped with went according to plan." But Miss Courteney was right—Miss Gibbon had been less than gracious as she'd left the night before, just minutes after Miss Courteney had begged off.

They reached the gates of the park and joined the line of carriages entering through the gate.

"So, I know you wrapped up your last show. What's next?" he asked, falling back on safe topics.

"You want information before it's available to the public?" She gasped mockingly and put a hand on her chest. "What next? Private performances?" she said, her voice low.

His face burned. He kept his eyes on the carriage in front of them. "Not as worried over your reputation as you led me to believe," he muttered under his breath.

"Hmm?" she asked, leaning closer to him. Her hand hovered near his elbow, as though she contemplated slipping her arm through his.

Shaking his head, he focused on the gravel path once more. "How can I be of help? Beyond financial support, I mean."

"You mean besides arranging interviews and filling my social calendar with gatherings you would rather not attend?"

Turning, he saw her smirk. A warmth spread from his cheeks to the tips of his ears and toes. She giggled, and his embarrassment receded, a small smile tugging at the corners of his lips.

"I am very grateful for the support you have shown us." Her voice was steady and serious now. Sincere.

Clearing his throat and expression, he changed the subject. He could not afford to examine his motives for helping her. "How are things at the theatre? Why were you so out of breath?"

She tucked a strand of hair, blown free in the light breeze, behind her ear and said, "We were rehearsing, and I lost track of the time. Our next show is *The Duke and the Dancer* by George Lemming."

"I'm not sure I know that one."

"It's a musical comedy. But I did not nab a lead role. Again."

"Would it help if I offered to finance the entire performance? I could stipulate that you receive a proper role for your talent."

"I appreciate the offer, but no. Mr. Martin makes the final casting decisions. I think he sometimes still sees me as the little girl he helped raise."

"You need to show him you've changed. Tell him up front what you deserve."

She shrugged. "I might not be good enough. Maybe I'm not what society wants."

He watched as she stared at her hands, playing with one finger on her glove. "I doubt that. Your last performance had me captivated. I do not offer my patronage to all and sundry. You are talented."

"Thanks for the confidence. I will try to do better."

He nudged her with his shoulder. "You don't have to try so hard."

"Stop." She laughed and put a hand up to cover her mouth until she'd finished. "You'll fill my head with ideas that I'm superior to everyone else, and I'll become insufferable."

"A true prima donna, then." When she looked up at him, he surprised them both by winking.

He was having too much fun to leave, but they could not drive forever. Especially with the gloomy clouds gathering overhead. He ought to get her back to the theatre. Ending their ride in the rain would be less than desirable. Much like the thought of her never performing as a star. She deserved to shine. She already did, in his eyes. How the rest of London could be so blind, he'd never know.

"You'll get the lead in the next play."

"I will. To prove you right."

They drove around the park until they exited back onto the street and he focused on navigating the phaeton.

"If you will direct me, I'll take you home."

A moment passed before she answered. "No, back to the theatre is fine. My father is still there. Maybe I'll be able to have a talk with Mr. Martin."

A carriage drove past them at a fast pace. His horses stamped their feet, so he clicked his tongue at them to keep them moving. "I think that's a good idea." He admired Miss Courteney. She knew what she wanted and took steps to accomplish her goals.

Miss Gibbon wanted for nothing. She did not have any ambition beyond marrying well. He did not see her settling for less than a duke. But becoming a duchess was not something one earned the way Miss Courteney worked to achieve her dreams.

They arrived at Drury Lane, the heavens still holding their piece, though rain was imminent. Jonathan studied how she held herself, her shoulders back, head high. Helping her out of the phaeton, he smiled at her.

"What?" she asked.

"Thank you for accompanying me."

"It was a much-needed break." She stared at the facade of the theatre and sighed but lost none of her strength.

"Go claim what you deserve."

"If my head fits through the door. You've blown it up so big." She grinned at him.

Realizing he still held her hand, he gave it a squeeze. "Goodbye, Miss Courteney." He placed a kiss on her hand.

Her eyes sparkled as she said, "Goodbye, Your Grace." She curtsied and slipped her fingers from his grasp and went inside the theatre.

Chapter 9

T HE WEEK AFTER HER drive with the duke found Isi trailing David around the theatre.

Isi's heart pounded as she tried to catch his attention. There was no leading lady in the prop cabinets. Nor would he find one in the dressing rooms.

Mary had contracted an illness of the lung. Weak from coughing fits, she planned to travel to Bath to see if the fresh air and restorative waters could help. Isi hoped that as the weather warmed with the arrival of April, that her friend's recovery would run smoothly.

She wasn't happy about Mary's illness, but she wouldn't waste such an opportunity. One she likely wouldn't have again.

David swiveled toward Isi after having a hurried conversation with the props master.

"*I'd-like-to-read-for-the-lead*." Her words slurred together, sounding like one word instead of seven.

"You what?" He skidded to a halt as she stepped in front of him.

"I believe I could carry the lead, if you'll allow me the chance to try."

He raised an eyebrow and looked her up and down, his lips clamped shut.

"I know my experience is limited, but I must perform to practice overcoming my weaknesses. I wish to be more than a supporting actress."

"Fine. Look over the lines. In the meantime, I'll be coming up with another play we could do—"

"I'm familiar with the opening scene. I could perform for you now."

Closing his mouth, he motioned to the stage. He chose a seat in the front row of the auditorium.

Isi took a deep breath and closed her eyes. She cleared her mind and body of the jitters that accompanied every performance. Then she recited the opening lines.

As she spoke, she became one with the character. She knew what came next without having to reach for the words. Straightening, she extended her arms out. Breathing deep in the diaphragm, she spoke until her voice filled the empty auditorium and everyone in the theatre had stopped to listen.

Not wanting to see what Martin thought, she focused on the empty chairs, imagining an attentive, captivated audience. Funny how only one face came to mind. A man with wavy brown hair and honey-brown eyes.

As the opening scene came to a close, she lowered her arms and peeked at Martin's stoic expression.

His eyebrows were no longer raised. He sat in the seat, arms crossed over his chest, mouth set in a line, indicating neither approval nor disapproval. His eyes bored into her as though trying to see her soul.

Clearing her throat, she said, "I need direction and—"

"The role is yours. I believe you'll excel." Standing, he snapped his fingers. "Anne!"

Anne approached, hands clasped in front of her.

"See that we fit the dresses to Isi's figure. You are right, Isi. Your recitation needs work, but that is why we rehearse."

Making his way up onto the stage, he came to stand in front of her. "Thank you for saving this production. I am proud to be working with you. You do your mother's legacy justice."

Isi's smile faded as he squeezed her hands, then walked away to continue working on the production. What advice would her mother have given her? Or would her words have been encouraging? She wrapped her arms around her middle, holding herself together.

A glance to the corner showed her father was once again in his cups, eyes glazed. With a sigh, she realized he hadn't noticed her performance.

The duke's face flashed through her mind again. What would his opinion of her performance have been? He would at least understand her longing for her mother.

As though she'd conjured him with her thoughts, he was there, walking through the aisles of the auditorium.

He slowed as she slipped off the stage, knowing her reputation was safe with the many people working nearby.

"I stopped by to invite you for another drive in the park." He jerked his thumb behind him. "The gentleman out front told me to come find you."

She nodded. "Mr. Bates has no time for anyone. He likes to act as busy as possible, even on the slow days without a show."

"So would you? Accompany me for a ride, that is."

"I would love to, but—"

"Isi, start running the lines for act two. We'll start rehearsing that first scene after lunch," David called from the back of the stage.

"I would enjoy a drive, but I don't have time."

His face and shoulders fell. "Of course. Perhaps in a few days." He turned to go.

A thrill ran through her as she touched his arm. "Wait. I got the lead. I'll be playing the role of the dancer who falls for the duke."

His eyes lit up as he faced her. "That's wonderful. How?"

"The part opened up, and I convinced David to give me a chance."

"He's not a fool. Congratulations." He scuffed his boot and stared at the ground, looking like a little boy trying to hide his feelings of disappointment. She knew he was pleased for her, but he'd been hoping to spend time with her.

She realized as he bowed and turned to go that she didn't want him to leave either.

"Maybe you could help me run lines?"

Turning back around, she noticed him trying to hold back his smile as his eyes danced happily. "I'd be delighted to, though you might have to tell me how exactly to help with that."

"I'll just fetch the script. It's really very simple. I practice my lines, and you get to read everybody else's." She heard him chuckle behind her as she turned to collect her pages for the first scene in act two. Retrieving her script from the table backstage where she'd set it earlier, she returned to the auditorium. With a glance around, she waved the duke up on stage. "Let's practice here. We'll be out of everyone's way while they work backstage or get something to eat."

"But still be properly chaperoned." He eyed Anne and Martin, who stood in the wings, watching them closely.

Isi shook her head with a smile and waved her hand at them to get on with their own business. "Exactly. Now then, you hold these, and I'll only look if I need to check a line. I'm not as familiar with this section of the play, as my previous character is not in this scene."

Shaking out the papers, he held them firmly in hand and cleared his throat. "Where should we start?"

"I'm playing the character of Odelia, so you'll read all of the other lines." She leaned over and pointed at the first line of the scene.

He straightened and delivered the line in a deep booming voice. Then hunching his shoulders, he bent forward and spoke in a shaky voice. When he crouched next and tried to speak with a falsetto, Isi couldn't hold her laughter in.

"What are you doing?" she gasped.

Standing quickly, he tugged on the hem of his jacket. "Performing. I don't know who these characters are, so I'm pretending one is a big burly man, one is an elderly gentleman, and the other is a little girl."

She clapped her hands.

"I just wanted to do the thing right," he grumbled. Frowning, he studied the script.

"You did a wonderful job. It was simply unexpected. *You* are unexpected." She bit her lip and clasped her hands behind her back, staring at the ground and feeling her cheeks pink up. Why had she said that?

"I'm unexpected?" She could hear the confusion in his voice but no anger, so he hadn't felt insulted.

Daring a glance up, she found him studying her, his brow drawn together, mouth turned slightly down.

"You're a duke. You must have a thousand things to do, yet here you are helping me run lines. You hate parties, yet you throw one for me anyway. To help my career, you enlist the help of a popular ladies' magazine. And you offered to be my patron, asking for nothing in return."

Even as she listed off the things he'd done for her, she couldn't believe anyone would care that much about her. Yet he had done all of those things, and what had she done? Accused him of being a lecherous rake and misjudged him time and time again.

His lips lifted in a small smile, and he shrugged. "I told you I think you have talent. It would be a shame if it went to waste." He shook the papers in his hands to straighten them. "Now, should we continue?"

"Only if you promise not to make me laugh again."

"That's not a promise I can keep. But I'll not do the voices if my acting skills are too distracting for you."

She chuckled and shook her head. "Read the lines however you like." As he began again, still differentiating between characters by using different voices, though more subdued than the first time through, Isi couldn't help thinking how lucky she was that he'd offered to be her patron and had continued to offer her support despite all the reasons she'd given him not to.

An hour passed in this manner, with him reading the other parts and making her laugh, but it seemed like mere minutes when David called the cast and crew together on the stage.

"Thank you." The duke handed back her script with a bow.

"For what?" The edges of the papers were still warm from his hands.

"I've always wondered if I would enjoy acting. Of course, such a thing is not a suitable pursuit for a duke, not outside of house parties and drawing rooms where it's all fun and games."

"Except I doubt you enjoy house parties."

He grimaced in horror and shook his head, making her laugh once again.

"This is as close as I'll ever get to acting on stage. It was an enjoyable experience." He bowed again and turned to leave. She followed him toward the edge of the stage, not wanting him to go.

"Perhaps we can practice together again sometime."

"I'd like that," he said over his shoulder.

"And of course, you'll come see the show. We open in a couple of weeks."

"I can't wait." He turned at the edge of the platform to face her once more and sighed. "I just wish I didn't have to bring anyone. Most people talk over the performance. That's why I insisted on a box nearest the stage so I could hear better."

She shrugged. "Come alone. You should be able to enjoy yourself."

His brows drew together as he considered her suggestion. "I would enjoy the show. And the actress in the lead role." He smiled, and heat raced through her body. "I'll think on it. I look forward to seeing your next performance."

She curtsied and watched him step down into the pit before walking up the aisles toward the exits. How could a man who'd been a stranger to her three weeks ago warm her heart and soul with simple words of praise? As he reached the doors, he opened them, then turn back, and even in the large dim room, she could see him wave to her.

Her heart jumped in her chest, and she waved back, waiting for the door to shut behind him before joining the others gathering around to begin rehearsal.

The duke had been so good to her. Yet there was nothing she could give him in return for his help. He needed nothing she had, and she had very little to give. But he'd repeatedly told her he enjoyed watching her performances. And now she was taking on a lead role. The only thing she could do to repay his kindness would be to give the performance of her life. She vowed then to work hard and make this her best performance yet.

Instead of imagining thousands of people clapping and cheering for her, she now pictured only one man whom she wanted to make smile more than anything.

Chapter 10

OPENING NIGHT OF ISI'S play found Jonathan in his box, alone as she had suggested, and enthralled. His chest swelled with pride despite having done nothing more than support Isi with monetary contributions.

Having heard the more familiar version of her name used at rehearsal weeks earlier, he could not think of her any other way, though she had not given him leave to use her given name, let alone a nickname.

She stood on the stage, her posture impeccable except for when she exaggerated her movements to look funny and cajole laughter from the audience.

Over the past few weeks, Jonathan had tended to estate business with his solicitor and kept himself busy in Lords. But even in moments when he needed to focus, his mind wandered to Drury Lane theatre. Though his distraction had been obvious to those around him, he hadn't heard whispers linking his name with Isi's in uncouth ways. Staying away kept any rumors from arising, so he forced himself to see to other tasks instead of seeking her out for a ride in the park or a dinner invitation. Instead, he'd kept his communications with her to a minimum, sending a note and some money with a footman.

As the curtains lowered for intermission, he sat back, blinking, awaking from a dream. The volume of chatter increased. The rustle of skirts drew his attention as members of the ton rose to mingle. Many were just arriving. He knew he had a duty to visit with acquaintances. Mother continually pressured him to choose a wife and secure the title and estate with an heir. But he couldn't bear the idea of having to speak with insipid girls such as Miss Gibbon. Not tonight.

Knowing what he wished for instead, he left his box and made his way through the crowds. Instead of stopping to chat, he waved and said a few words when necessary until he reached the door that led backstage. A sign said *Acting Company Only*, but he ignored it and slipped through, closing the door behind him. He moved through the hall until he reached a bustling center where people carried props and sets to and fro in a manic fashion. Others stood around drinking or rehearsing lines.

He saw Isi's father slumped on a stool in a corner, an almost empty bottle in his hands. The man swigged the remaining contents before belching it out. Liquid dribbled down his chin and soaked into his stained shirt.

Searching, his eyes lit on her, and he felt his shoulders relax amidst the chaos.

Just beyond the door stood his peers and acquaintances. To them, only status mattered. Thus, appearances mattered to him. Most intermissions were spent waiting for a chance to retake his seat and immerse himself in the performance once again. Anything to turn attention from himself.

But tonight, just seeing Isi, his rigid posture slackened. His breathing slowed. Taking in her flushed face and the wisps of curls that framed her cheeks made him smile.

He strode toward her, chest puffed out. Their eyes met as she smoothed the front of her dress. Her face lit with a smile.

Reaching up to play with a ringlet draped over her shoulder, she dipped her head. "What do you think of the show?"

"You are mesmerizing. I couldn't keep my eyes off you."

A blush appeared on her cheeks, and she bit her lip. "Truly?"

When he nodded, her color deepened and she glanced down, scuffing her shoe along the ground. She was enchanting. Nothing in her demeanor struck him as fake or rehearsed the way some young ladies appeared.

Behind them, someone called the actors and actresses to their places for the next scene, and she glanced over her shoulder as she turned to take her place. "I have to go. Thank you for coming. And for visiting me back here. I was wondering if I would see you tonight."

He nodded his head, but reached out, his fingers skimming her arm as she passed.

She turned, and their eyes met. "I'll see you after the show as well," he murmured.

With a curtsy she said, "I look forward to seeing you, Your Grace." Then she hurried off toward the stage. He reached his box a minute into the next scene.

The second half of the play, Isi exuded a warm glow. Her lines were spot on, delivered clearly and with perfect timing to have maximum comedic effect.

Occasionally, her eyes flickered to his box. Each time, his grin grew and his chest rose with the pounding of his heart.

Near the end of the play, he left his box, hoping to slip backstage without notice. He had no desire to converse with anyone, but he also couldn't have rumors flying about him and a certain actress for whom he was acting as patron. Neither did she want her name dragged through the mud. Which was yet another quality that drew him to her.

She had the tenacity to work hard at her passion along with decorum and a wish that society view her as a lady. If society counted her as one of them, then spending time together wouldn't raise any eyebrows. Or so he told himself.

As he slipped backstage, he watched from the wings while Isi delivered her last lines and the curtains closed.

The muffled applause penetrated the thick fabric, and the curtains parted again so the audience could share their enthusiasm for a woman he knew had brought a smile to many.

Still, she looked up at his box, and for a moment, her shoulders fell. She recovered as she curtsied for the adoring audience.

Then she turned and walked off the stage, hanging her head as she reached the darkened space.

"You were magnificent," he said as she drew near.

Her head shot up and her eyes sparkled. "I thought you'd gone."

"I told you I would see you after the show."

She shrugged. "People say a lot of things." Glancing around, her eyes landed on her father, and she sighed as her shoulders crumpled. "Case in point."

Before she could explain, several other troupe members came up to speak with her, and Jonathan stepped back, leaning against the wall. Nearby, her father began snoring, his chin butting against his chest. The man had missed the whole show. His daughter's debut in a lead role she had fought for, and he hadn't the decency to forgo drinking for one night.

Something had to be done. But would the man accept Jonathan's help?

As he stood nearby, contemplating Isi's father and wondering how he might assist the man, Isi approached. She'd changed out of her costume. Her demeanor was light, but creases on her forehead belied her concern.

"I'm sorry I got pulled away. Thank you so much for coming." Her focus rested on her father, and she frowned before turning more fully to face him. "Was it terrible having to watch the show alone?"

He shook his head. "One my best experiences at the theatre. It justified the cost of my box."

"Wonderful." Wringing her hands, she eyed her father. "Shall I walk you out? I'm sure they'll have pulled around your carriage by now."

"I'll see you both home." He stepped toward her father, but she held up a hand.

"We'll be fine."

"As a gentleman and your patron, I cannot in good conscience leave you to fend for yourself. Not again." His gaze lingered over her small frame, wondering how she managed on her own. Tearing his attention from her earnest expression, he hauled her father's arm up around his shoulders and hooked his other arm around the man's waist.

"Quickest way to the street?"

"This way." She led him to an exit onto the street behind the theatre.

"Look. A coach." She waved her hand in the direction of a hackney near the corner. "I shall hire him, and if you'll help put my father inside, I can take it from there."

Jonathan shook his head. "It is late, and I'm no cad. I'll not abandon you now. Come, my carriage can't be far." He began walking around the building. Isi's slower steps meant she trailed behind him and her father.

"Ah, there." His was one of the few carriages left outside of the theatre. Jonathan headed for it, supporting her father's weight. The man's head lolled toward him, wheezing. Jonathan turned away and held his breath.

The driver, seeing them coming, hopped off his seat and opened the door, then stood by awaiting instructions. It pleased Jonathan that the man didn't ask stupid questions or even show surprise that a drunkard and a stunning young lady accompanied him.

Jonathan forced Isi's father into the carriage, where he slumped on the bench.

"Where to?" he asked Isi, gesturing to the driver standing a pace away.

Isi bit her lip as though debating with herself before giving the address, avoiding his eye.

Then Jonathan held out his hand for Isi.

She glanced around before taking his hand and sitting on the bench opposite the one occupied by her father. His limbs sprawled across the cushions, leaving no room for her.

Jonathan turned to the driver but snapped his mouth shut as Mr. Drew approached from down the street. "Your Grace, I thought I spotted you alone in your box this evening."

Barely inclining his head in the man's direction, he said, "I came to enjoy the performance." Hoping to stave off any further conversation he opened his mouth to speak to his driver again, but Mr. Drew spoke first.

"Ah, to inspect your investment? I heard you were acting as patron for one of the ladies in this company."

"Indeed." Short, gruff answers sometimes deterred more conversation, but apparently Mr. Drew could not take a hint.

Glancing into the carriage, Mr. Drew lowered his voice. "And were you satisfied with the lady's performance?"

"More than. Now if you'll excuse me, please give your mother my regards." With one last dip of his head, Jonathan turned his back on Mr. Drew. Once he heard retreating footsteps, Jonathan spoke to the driver. "There is extra coin for you if you keep your mouth shut about this around the gossipmongers." He motioned with his head toward Isi and her unconscious father.

"Yes, Your Grace." The man waited for Jonathan to enter the carriage, shutting the door behind him.

Jonathan hesitated only a moment before seating himself beside Isi. Her father had taken over the other bench, drool pooling on the cushions. Though he tried to keep his distance, the space was smaller than he'd thought, and his leg brushed her skirts, his arm just bouncing against hers.

"Thank you for your help," said Isi after a few moments.

"Of course. It is the least I can do after your magnificent performance. You deserve better." He cleared his throat, hoping he hadn't said too much.

"So you enjoyed the show?"

"I did. You were born for the stage."

"My mother was an actress." He could not see her face, but her voice spoke of longing.

"Do you miss her?"

"Do you miss your father?" He felt her angle her body to face him.

"Yes." His voice rasped. So many times in the past few years, he'd doubted himself. Wondering what his father would say about Miss Gibbon or many other eligible young women. Would he have married earlier? Produced an heir by now? Would his father have approved?

He guessed his father would have liked Isi. Who wouldn't? But was she far enough beneath him in status that even knowing his feelings, his father might have discouraged the connection?

One glance at the sleeping form across the carriage confirmed his uncertainties. The Duke of Edston could never be connected to a drunkard.

And yet, Jonathan could not help but compare Isi to Miss Gibbon. One was part of the social elite, an upstanding specimen of a woman and one who could have her pick of suitors. The other an actress, having to work for her living, supporting a father one couldn't even mention in polite company.

The man exuded the smell of cheap, stale ale from every pore, filling the carriage.

Still, with the soft rustling of skirts beside him, he hadn't felt so comfortable and at peace since before his father had died.

"Was your mother as talented as you?"

Isi shrugged. "I was young when she passed. I started performing when I was a child. Most of my time was spent bouncing around backstage, making mischief between my scenes. I don't remember watching her perform. But the troupe speaks well of her."

"And your father? Was he an actor?"

"In his youth, he was. His father ran a troupe as well. My parents met while producing *Romeo and Juliet*." She sighed. "He used to enjoy the work."

The carriage slowed and then rocked to a stop. Jonathan waited until the door opened before stepping out. The neighborhood was dark, the buildings stark silhouettes. The stench of the street mixed with the dampness from rains earlier in the evening curled his nose hairs.

Around a corner, a cat meowed, and Jonathan fought the urge to cover his mouth and nose with his sleeve. "This place?"

Isi stepped into the carriage doorway.

"Unfortunately." She sighed.

He held out a hand for Isi.

"I know it's dirty and beneath your dignity to be here. I'll just help my father inside, and you can be on your way."

Jonathan shook his head and stretched out his arms to adjust the shoulders of his jacket. "Absolutely not. I shall escort your father to his room." He reached into the carriage and pulled her father from the dark interior toward the door. The man hung limp from his hands, and his arms felt the strain of his unsupported weight. Grunting, he lowered the man to the street and wrapped an arm around his waist.

Isi stood watching him before turning on her heel and leading him inside an even darker hall than the already dark street. The windows were grimy, further limiting the light.

"This way," she whispered, and he followed her footsteps in the dark, feeling each step forward with his toes to avoid bumping into furniture.

"Is that you, Miss Courteney?" asked a woman as they began climbing a set of stairs.

"Yes, my father and me."

"Who's that with you?"

"Nobody. I'm exhausted after the performance. I'll see you in the morning." The woman must be her landlady.

Jonathan knew it was irrational. Isi couldn't tell the woman the Duke of Edston was supporting her unconscious father.

Still, he hoped she didn't think he was a nobody.

Chapter 11

"JUST IN THERE." Isi pushed open a door and stepped back.

The duke heaved Papa through the doorway and lowered him onto his bed.

Papa snorted, and Isi cringed. He couldn't have let her have this one night to revel in the feelings of success that performing onstage had stirred within her. No, he'd had to celebrate her opening night, and he'd started before the curtains had even risen.

The duke stepped out of the room and back into the hall.

She squared her shoulders, not willing to let her dignity slip.

"Listen, as your patron, might I find you and your father lodgings closer to the theatre?" His voice was quiet, the timbre of his voice low, and she wished she could accept. But she shook her head.

"Thank you, but we are fine where we are. It's not so bad. And you must keep up appearances."

"How can I call myself a patron of the arts? If people discovered you live here—"

She held up a hand and then realizing he couldn't see her in the dark, she stepped forward, placing her hand on his chest.

"If you moved my father and I into a nicer place, they'd call me a kept woman—and much worse. Then who would have either of us?"

71

She tilted her head and tried not to focus on the warmth she felt in her fingertips.

He did not speak, and she tapped the spot above his heart, intending to pull away.

One of his hands pinned hers against his chest, and he shifted closer to her.

"What if what they think isn't the most important thing?" he whispered.

She closed her eyes, feeling his breath stirring the wisps of hair that had escaped the knot at the back of her head. Her mind shouted to push him away, to hide in her room, shut and lock the door. If anyone found them, she would have no future.

Yet her heart kept her rooted in place even as he rested his hand on the back of her neck, his thumb caressing her ear.

She slid her hands up his chest, wrapping her arms around his neck.

He lowered his head toward hers, his breath whispering over her mouth.

And then his lips found hers, and all thoughts flew from her mind. Her neck burned where his hand touched skin. Heart racing, pounding against her ribs, she felt herself fall against him. Her chest tightened with a lack of air, and still she wanted more. She curled one hand into the hair at the nape of his neck. Raising up on tiptoes, she clutched his collar and pulled him closer.

All she wanted was to stay wrapped up in him. To hear him tell her she was magnificent and to support him when society demanded he socialize.

The warmth of his mouth on hers lingered for a long moment after they broke apart, each gasping to catch their breath. Her head swirled until she remembered where they were. Standing at the top of the stairs in her dingy lodgings. She forced herself to step back, clasping her hands in front of her.

"You need to go. Thank you. For coming tonight," she clarified, her lips still tingling, face burning. "And for escorting my father and me home. Really, I can't thank you enough. Your Grace." She curtsied when she remembered who he was and the power and influence he wielded.

When he spoke, his breath was heavy, and she forced the feel of his lips from her mind. "As you wish. Good night, Isi."

She wished she could see his face. What was he thinking? His voice had been soft. Was he hurt? By her rejection or the fact that he knew she was right? They couldn't be together. Entertaining such thoughts could damage both of their reputations. While society overlooked his indiscretions, they would brand her, leaving her no chance of flourishing on stage.

She would fade into obscurity, just another actress with loose morals.

His footsteps on the stairs matched the pounding of her heart, and she listened as the carriage drove away before she could force her feet, heavy and dragging, to move into her room.

As she readied herself for bed, she forced herself to consider her performance, trying to ignore the other memories she'd made tonight.

Rubbing a palm along her collarbone, she tried to ease the ache that had sprung up, a hollow feeling in her chest. Swallowing, she wandered in the dark over to her water basin. Cupping her hands, she splashed water on her face then sipped, trying to swallow the thick lump in her throat.

To attain more lead roles, she needed to be outstanding. Otherwise, she and her father could never escape this place.

Something scratched along the trim and floorboards. Isi lacked the energy to shudder over the creeping creature.

The duke was a distraction. His money was helpful—needed, even—but despite their kiss, they could never be more. Neither she, nor society, would allow it.

Chapter 12

T HE DAY AFTER ISI'S performance, Jonathan's mother insisted they go visiting.

Normally, he refused and sequestered himself away for the rest of the day, either at his club or the House of Lords.

But he didn't have the energy to wage battle with his mother, so he slouched beside her in the carriage. Water dripped from the roof, and they splashed through puddles on the road.

"Don't look so severe when we arrive, please," his mother sniffed.

Jonathan grimaced but tried his best not to frown as they arrived. The butler showed them into the parlour.

Miss Gibbon and her mother, Lady Gibbon, stood as they entered and curtsied, greeting them both.

"How are you both this morning?" Lady Gibbon asked gesturing for them to seat themselves in the chair across from where they stood.

"I'm doing well. Jonathan got in late last night. He's wishing I had let him sleep this morning. Especially with this weather." His mother grinned at him while taking her seat.

Lady Gibbon blinked her large eyes quickly before rounding her owlish gaze on him. "What kept you out so late?"

He avoided meeting her gaze as he sat, adjusting his coat. "I went to the theatre." Looking up after several seconds silence, Jonathan saw the end of a shared look between the Gibbon women, a smug look of vindication combined with a hint of concern. Concern for him?

"With whom? Did you see Miss Bedelia? I believe she said she was going."

"I did not."

"Was the performance sublime?"

"Indeed. Miss Courteney played the lead role and captured my attention."

Miss Gibbon and her mother exchanged another look. "Perhaps you'll have to go again. I should love to watch the performance, but Father refuses to pay for a box."

Jonathan hoped his mother or Lady Gibbon would change the subject. Instead, the three of them just stared at him, Miss Gibbon fluttering her eyelashes.

Fighting the urge to roll his eyes, he said, "I'd be delighted to accompany you to the show. It was captivating."

Sitting there, Jonathan watched as the three women conversed, prodding him for an answer or comment. His mother sat straight and still. She never raised her voice and always covered her mouth or tempered her smile, even as Miss Gibbon told an amusing story about a dandy at Miss Bedelia's last dinner party.

In the telling, Miss Gibbon kept her hands folded in her lap. The volume of her voice never rose, and her expression did not change. Though she smiled, he wondered how funny she thought the story was. No emotion crossed her mother's face.

And yet, his father had married his mother. Miss Gibbon knew the impossible standards to which people held a duke and his family. She welcomed that life. Just as his mother had when marrying Father.

But as he watched Miss Gibbon converse, he imagined the way Isi would tell the same story. She would play up the ridiculous outfit the man had worn, how he had flicked every speck of dust off his turquoise blue coat. Her smile would be radiant. Big enough that everyone in the audience would see it no matter their proximity to the stage.

But such a loud and exaggerated retelling was unbecoming for a duchess.

"She is darling. A little too interested in a career on stage." Miss Gibbon wrinkled her nose.

"Who?" Jonathan shook free of his thoughts with a sinking feeling.

"Miss Courteney," said his mother before turning to the Gibbon women. "While it's true her ambition for the stage is her only aspiration, she's hardly in a position to want more. We must remember not everyone is as fortunate as we are."

Jonathan's heart warmed at hearing his mother defending Miss Courteney. Until he realized she only saw her as an actress, not a suitable daughter-in-law.

"So true. Although...there were rumors. I mean, I'm not a gossip, but one hears things." Lady Gibbon's eyes drifted to Jonathan before blinking and peering at his mother.

"Please tell me you don't believe them." His mother shook her head and sent an exasperated smile his way.

He frowned, his brows drawing together. "What rumors?"

"Some are wondering if your...*patronage* might be something more." Lady Gibbon raised an eyebrow.

Snorting in disbelief, he sat up straight. "They are mistaken. Miss Courteney is nothing but proper, and I would never sully a lady's reputation." His mouth drew into a grim line as he watched Lady Gibbon and her daughter glance at each other. They didn't believe him. He had to set the record straight—Isi's reputation was in his hands.

"I have no intention—"

"Of course you don't." Miss Gibbon cut him off and sent a placating smile his way before turning to his mother. "We don't put stock in what other people say. As mother said, we simply heard rumors and wondered if you were aware of them. Don't worry yourselves over them. No one important puts any stock in such things."

"May I ask where you heard these...lies?" Jonathan asked through gritted teeth.

"Well, Mrs. Drew was here earlier. According to her son, you and Miss Courteney left the theatre together last night." Miss Gibbon's eyes narrowed marginally.

"Along with Mr. Courteney, her father. As her patron, rather than allow them to travel home in a hired carriage, I offered them a ride." The addition of her father should alleviate any concerns about them being unchaperoned. He knew from the lines forming on Mother's brow that she was worried over his reputation.

Jonathan forced his balled hands to grip the arms of the chair in an attempt to appear more relaxed.

"Ah, Mr. Drew must have failed to mention that detail to his mother." Mrs. Gibbon didn't appear pleased, more like appeased. No doubt she'd been worried that her daughter's prospects of making a match with him were in jeopardy due to an inevitable scandal.

"As I said, no one of any standing would believe such lies. Not if they are at all acquainted with you." Miss Gibbon tilted her head and sent another smile his way, but her flirting only prickled Jonathan further. His knuckles whitened, tightening around the chair.

Mother picked up on his frustration and rose with a sigh.

"We ought to be off. It was lovely to see you both."

"Do not forget you promised to accompany me to the theatre for the newest showing. I shall hold you to it." Miss Gibbon made her demand seem demure, but it grated on Jonathan's nerves, and he fought to smile at her and nod his head in approval as propriety demanded.

He and his mother exited the house. As they entered the carriage and his mother gave the driver another address, he realized the Gibbons were only the first family with a daughter of marrying age out in society whom his mother planned to visit that day.

Once seated inside, she adjusted her gloves.

"That went well. Miss Gibbon has blossomed this year. She was such a flighty thing when she made her debut."

He took his cues from her and avoided discussing the topic weighing heavily on his mind. "As I recall, she was only sixteen. I think exuberance in a girl so young is excusable."

With a subtle lift to her chin, his mother said, "I disagree. Those with long memories—"

"Such as yours?" He arched an eyebrow, and she smiled.

"We do not forget first impressions. And they can be very important when making life-altering decisions."

He felt the tension in his shoulders hunch at her obvious insinuation to marriage. "I'm glad to discover you no longer think Miss Gibbon a suitable option for the role of my wife. I shall take measures to put off my engagement to take her to the theatre. Forever, if possible."

His mother tsked. "That is not what I said. As I began, she has changed and matured into a wonderful young lady of good breeding."

"And if you were to choose, we would wed within the season."

"Maybe just after it ends. In the country? To usher out the season, lead in the new."

He rested his arm on the window's edge and rubbed his lip as he looked outside, wondering for the hundredth time what his father would say if he knew how often his son's thoughts turned from ladies of good breeding and status to a lowly actress and her drunken father.

Jonathan could pretend away her flaws, the ones society would pick at if given the chance, but he could do nothing about her father. They would never accept him. If Jonathan joined his family name with theirs, it would cast a shadow on him and his descendants that, as his mother pointed out, might stretch far into the future.

Unless her father cleaned up his act. Perhaps the man just needed a push in the right direction. Someone to guide him away from the drink and show him that his daughter's future was in his hands and a worthy reason to start living his life as the man he used to be.

Even if her father did clean up his act, society still wouldn't accept Isi. Not in the way he wished they would. Jonathan's continued presence near her would only damage both of their reputations.

Even though his mother filled his day with visits to every young lady with any merit, he couldn't get Isi's shining ringlets and sparkling eyes out of his mind. Despite his thoughts, he needed to keep his distance. If not for himself, then for her reputation. That was the best way for him to help further her career, he decided upon reflection. Yes, distance would be for the best.

Chapter 13

W ITH THE ARRIVAL OF May came the sun. Though Isi felt the mild warmth in the air on her skin, nothing could warm her through. She hadn't seen or heard from the duke in three weeks. Not that she'd been counting. He was a busy and important man, after all.

No, she simply knew how long it had been because tonight was the last night of the troupe's performance of *The Duke and the Dancer*. Isi entered the theatre from the back alley. There would be no rehearsals today. David had called a meeting to plan for their next show, which would begin its run after a different troupe's performances at the Drury Lane Theatre.

David stood before them and nodded at her but didn't ask after Papa's whereabouts.

She wouldn't have anything to tell him if he had. Her father had not been in his rooms when she'd gone to check on him this morning. Guessing at which pub he was frequenting that week would be like taking a shot in the dark. It was likely he'd had to move further afield than usual unless he'd found some way to pay off his tabs at the pubs nearest their rooms.

Clearing his throat and clapping his hands to silence the conversations around them, David began the meeting. "We shall perform *A Midsummer Night's Dream* next."

Isi smiled as the rest of the troupe reacted favorably. Shakespeare's playful and faerie-filled romp through the woods at night fit very well with their troupe's style of performance. Not to mention it was her favorite of the bard's plays. Perhaps the day was looking up, as the sunshine outside indicated.

"If you want a specific part, see me and we can discuss it. I have some idea of whom to cast, but Isi has shown us that I can be wrong."

A few people chuckled and then began discussing the play.

Isi stepped toward David, who folded his arms and studied her, his eyes alight with amusement. "Here to demand your next part already?"

"You said if we had someone specific in mind..." She trailed off until he nodded for her to continue.

"I want the part of Helena, if that's possible." She winced at herself for adding the last bit, instead of putting on a show of confidence.

"Not Hermia? Or Titania, even?" His eyes were wide with surprise.

She shook her head. "Helena has a depth to explore, whereas Hermia's story is written and told before the play really begins. And Titania isn't as playful or comic as you know I prefer."

He rubbed his chin and nodded. "I suppose you're right. I will consider your request."

"Thank you." She'd turned to speak with a costumer when movement at the corner of her eye caught her attention.

The duke stood not far away, watching her with a solemn look.

Her eyes darted about, only half-hoping they might need her for something somewhere else. Pulling on her ear, she took a breath, but it caught in her chest.

Then he was before her. He held his hand out as she curtsied, and she placed her hand in his, feeling her cheeks heat as he raised it to his lips. Her eyes sought his, and she felt trapped in their depth, his emotions swirling just below the surface.

Her thoughts flickered back to their kiss, the way she'd felt in his arms, whole, peaceful, wanted. Had he felt those things too? And if so, why had he stayed away so long?

Clearing her throat, she smiled. "To what do I owe this pleasure, Your Grace?"

"I went to your home for a visit, but your landlady told me you were out. I assumed you would be here."

"Did you need something?"

"No," he shook his head and clasped his hands behind his back. "I went by to deliver more money. I paid your rent for the next few months. Yours and your father's." He huffed and glanced at his shoes. "I wanted to see you."

"Thank you again for your patronage," she said, hating how she felt at needing him to help pay her bills.

"Why are you here so early? Surely you don't need to rehearse."

Shaking her head, she said, "We are discussing our next show."

"May I ask what it will be?"

Glancing around, she lowered her voice and said, "Only if you promise not to reveal it to anyone."

"On my honor." He held up his right hand, and she smiled.

"*A Midsummer Night's Dream.*"

"Ah, Shakespeare. I look forward to it."

"As do I. I think Helena has the most comedic potential."

"Do you not think Titania the more regal part?"

"She is Queen of the Faeries, but she is too severe."

"Perhaps if you played her, she would not seem so."

"But I do not wish to play Titania. I have asked David for Helena's part, and I hope to get it." She bit the inside of her cheek, annoyed though at him for staying away, or at this conversation she couldn't say.

"As your patron, may I not voice my opinion?"

She dipped her head, but held eye contact. A small voice inside her mind questioned why she had so much confidence around this man, who could influence society with a look, while with David she faltered. What was it about the duke that seemed to give her an inner strength and the courage to use it?

"While Helena can be played as a bit of a jester, she could also be seen as a sad commentary on women who are desperate. Again that desperation can be funny, but I believe such cruel humor is beneath you."

"That is not how I see her at all. She fights for herself, something women are hardly allowed to do, but she does meet with trouble along the way and in such moments, in the play as in life, we have two options. To laugh or to cry."

She straightened and took a step away from him, hoping the distance would help her feel less betrayed. She'd hoped he would join her in excitement over the role she'd chosen. Despite his help paying her rent, she would not allow him to dictate to her. Far too much rode on her career. His patronage was unlikely to last forever, and if she let him tell her which parts she should take now, it may set a dangerous precedent that could ruin her career.

By taking less comedic roles now, she would have an average career filled with many different roles instead of a name that stood for something the way Mrs. Siddons' did.

"Let's not argue, please Isi." He sighed.

"I do not wish to, but I must point out that I have not given you leave to call me by my Christian name, nor any version of it."

The hurt that flashed across his face was brief. She wished she could take back the comment. Too often, she spoke her mind before thinking about what was best. Still, she hadn't seen the man in weeks. And despite the fact that she'd come to think of him as a friend, she knew all too well how society would look at their friendship. If anyone heard him calling her Isi, her reputation would be blackened beyond repair, her career over in a moment.

He lowered his head in acknowledgment and glanced around them at the rest of her troupe as though remembering they were not alone. "I look forward to seeing your next show, then. It will likely be the last before I remove to Edston Manor for the summer."

Isi felt her eyes widen and dipped her head, hiding her expression as she curtsied again. Of course, he would be leaving Town. All the wealthy families and those in Lords were. Still, she hadn't expected that she wouldn't see him again for months. Schooling her face into what she hoped was a neutral expression, she looked up, but he was gone.

Chapter 14

L ATER THAT EVENING, JONATHAN found himself seated across from Miss Gibbon in his carriage, accompanying her and her mother to the last performance of *The Duke and the Dancer*. She fanned herself and smiled at him over the fan's lace edge.

"Did I tell you the Heathertons are coming?"

He nodded. Though he wished he hadn't, he'd given her leave to invite any of her friends to fill his box. There were just enough seats for the people she'd listed. He knew most of them but dreaded spending an extended period trapped with them.

His purpose in allowing her to fill the box had been in the vain hope that her guests would divide her attention, leaving little time for him. Unfortunately, it also meant he was tasked with playing the part of host to her hostess.

Staring out the windows of the rocking carriage, he watched as people strolled along the sidewalks and other vehicles jostled for position on the street outside of the theatre's entrance. He refused to dwell on everything he could not have.

The bright spot was that he could watch Isi do what she did best.

Or rather Miss Courteney, as he repeatedly reminded himself. Not Isi. Not to him.

Shaking off such thoughts, he waited for the carriage to stop before exiting. Helping the ladies from the carriage, he reminded himself with whom he'd come and the reasons behind his actions.

Society had noticed his infatuation with Miss Courteney. For both their sakes, he needed to distance himself from her. His reputation, though unscathed now, would only come away with minor scratches when compared to Isi's if anyone thought she was his mistress.

He knew she valued her reputation and smiled at the memory of their first meeting and the unfortunate misunderstanding between the two of them.

Miss Gibbon caught his eye, and he shook his head as he offered her his arm, escorting her into the building among the other lords and ladies attending the performance.

"I do hope we aren't too early. I usually arrive after the first act. It takes up so much time, and nothing seems to happen."

He nodded at Miss Gibbon's observation, though his nerves grated. The beginning set up everything that went on in succeeding acts. One could not enjoy a performance without being present for the exposition.

Reminding himself that Miss Gibbon did not attend the theatre to enjoy the performance but rather to see and be seen, he glanced around for someone else with whom she could converse. The dull throbbing in his head had erupted into a full headache.

"Ah, there's Miss Lancing. I should invite her to join us."

"You invited so many others, I believe the seats are filled. But as it is early, not everyone has arrived. Perhaps she could join us for a time." Yet another reason he would never marry Miss Gibbon. The effort involved with arranging entertainment for her was draining, and he couldn't imagine having the stamina to avoid his wife all the time. Some couples lived apart, but he had no desire to hurt Miss Gibbon by suggesting such an arrangement.

They made their way through the crowd to greet Miss Lancing, who declined their offer to join them as she was on her way to the Earl of Sotheby's box, at his invitation. The twinkle in her eye indicated she hoped to make a match with the young earl. Jonathan pitied the man.

So many women had designs on men of wealth and title. The status was all they desired. Jonathan knew men with both a wife and a wife in watercolors. But the energy one put into keeping a mistress happy was not worth it, especially when just as much energy went into assuring the happiness and comfort one's wife and children.

Focusing on one woman was easier. One who wanted him for more than his money and title.

But the one who occupied his every waking thought could never be his.

Sighing, he led Miss Gibbon, her mother trailing behind them, to his box. Sitting in the seat that afforded him the best view of the stage, Jonathan watched the performance.

They had indeed missed the first act, and Miss Courteney was below, shining as only an actress with her talent could.

For a moment, their eyes met. He smiled until he noticed a shadow cross her face before she turned back to the audience and attempted to continue her performance, though she stumbled.

Just then the Heathertons, and a few of Miss Gibbon's other guests joined them.

He greeted the others stiffly and attempted to keep up the conversation. Although he felt a pull toward the stage, he ignored the performance. Miss Gibbon fluttered her eyelashes at him and laughed at everything he said. It took all of his self-control not to snap at her to stop her insipid giggling. Gritting his teeth, he smiled through it.

By the end of the show, the group was boisterous. None of them followed the plot. Jonathan felt sorry for Isi. This group was not an anomaly. When they left, they might discuss the jewels someone wore with the wrong color or cut of gown. Or the rake who flirted with a young girl fresh to the season. No one would recall the actors. Some wouldn't even be able to name the play.

Leaving an impression with an audience couldn't be easy. Despite ignoring the performance, Jonathan's heart jumped at the sound of her voice. He breathed easier in her presence.

As he felt the weight of Miss Gibbon's hand on his arm, he realized that, despite his best efforts, his thoughts had never been far from Isi.

"Thank you for tonight. I had a wonderful time. And what a pair we made as host and hostess. I believe this was the most successful performance either of us has attended in quite some time." Miss Gibbon smiled up at him, her eyes sparkling as though they shared a brilliant victory.

He held back a sigh as he helped her into the carriage. "Yes, it was quite a performance tonight," he said, climbing in across from Miss Gibbon and her mother once again, wishing she'd meant Isi's performance instead of her own.

Chapter 15

IT SURPRISED ISI WHEN the duke pulled up in a carriage in front of her rented rooms the morning after her last performance. Before she could examine her feelings, she noticed the duke's companion. Papa sat beside him, laughing and gesturing with his hands the way he did when telling a story.

She schooled her face into what she hoped was a pleasant smile, but inside, her emotions raged. The duke's attendance at the theatre the night before had unsettled her. The tips of her ears burned, remembering the sight of Miss Gibbon hanging on his arm.

The man was her patron, nothing more. They couldn't even call one another friends. She knew her place. It could never be beside him. Society had accepted a few actresses to their ranks as wives to peers. But never to a duke.

She did not want society to shun her. She wanted them to adore her, to applaud her, to hold the entire audience captivated, if only for a moment.

The duke alighted from his phaeton and nodded at her as she curtsied, cementing in her mind her proper place. Father stepped down behind him and clapped an arm on the duke's shoulder as he finished his story about a time long past when he'd performed on stage.

What was the duke doing with her father? She'd assumed Papa was sleeping in a pub or the street somewhere, too drunk to find his way home after going out to celebrate the end of the play the night before.

"To what do I owe this pleasure, Your Grace?" She called his attention to her, tipping her chin up a notch and clasping her hands in front of her.

"I hoped you would have time for a ride in the park."

"Whatever for? Your other friends hadn't the time?"

He winced. She felt a slight pang before remembering how it had felt to see him ignoring the play, ignoring her.

"Isi," Papa snapped. "Manners. Sorry, Your Grace. She takes after her mother's sharp tongue."

Waving his hand in the air to shoo away her father's concern that he'd taken offense, the duke turned his gaze on her once more. "It is not their company I desire." His brown eyes darkened further.

With a sigh, she looked at the ground and fidgeted with her gloves. "Very well."

He handed her up into the vehicle and then climbed up beside her, urging on the horses.

They were quiet as they drove through the streets until they reached the park.

It was early for the throngs who descended at the fashionable hour. A few people strolled about, but only one other carriage meandered ahead of them.

"Will you rehearse with your troupe for the new show over the next few weeks?"

She nodded. "David should finalize the cast list in a few days. Then we'll receive our scripts and start learning lines."

"And did you ask for Hermia's part? Or Titania's perhaps?"

"No." The hairs on her arms prickled and she frowned. "I told you, I asked to play the part of Helena."

"But we discussed that Helena's part is undesirable. She's less of a leading role and not fit for the Queen of Comedy."

"I disagree." She felt him stiffen beside her and turned so she was further away from him, but facing him more. "I think, in many instances, Helena is the only comedic relief. Oberon and Titania's quarrels aren't amusing, nor do I wish to play opposite a man wearing the head of an ass. As for Hermia, I told you, her part holds no mystery. It is obvious to me, from the beginning, that she and Lysander will have a happy ending together."

"You would rather play a silly girl, chasing after an absurd man who doesn't recognize a good thing standing right in front of him?"

"At least Helena is true to herself and what she wants."

"At her own expense. It's ridiculous that she chases after a man. Especially when he professes he does not, will not, cannot love her."

His voice had risen, and Isi felt he aimed his words at her rather than the fictional character she hoped to play.

Matching his volume, she said, "You're right. She is ridiculous for thinking a man so far above her station could love her back."

Reaching over, she pulled on the reins until the phaeton came to a stop. Clutching her skirts, she jumped, stumbling away from the carriage, across the damp grass, and out of the park.

Chapter 16

J ONATHAN WATCHED AS ISI ran from the park. A glance around showed that several people were watching their exchange. He felt the heat in his cheeks as he tried to maneuver the phaeton out to follow her, but by the time he reached the entrance through which she had exited, she was nowhere in sight.

Which direction had she gone?

He chose one and pulled out onto the street, his eyes scanning for any sign of her. He knew his odds of finding her were slim when he reached a crossroads and didn't see her.

Instead, he drove home, feeling the heat in his cheeks dissipate.

Their fight had felt personal. It hadn't felt like a patron speaking with his artist on how to best further her career. He'd only meant to encourage her to take the best parts.

Helena was a stupid girl chasing after an even more foolish man. Demetrius professed his love to Helena based solely on her father's encouragement.

He handed his phaeton and horses over to the stable master, then went searching for Mother. The best alternative to conversing with Father was asking her opinion.

Even knowing what she would say, he needed to hear that he could never pursue Isi. Then he could settle for someone more proper. Such as Miss Gibbon.

His steps faltered as he considered life married to Miss Gibbon. Parties and balls would abound, they would hardly ever be alone, and when they were, she would talk his ear off. A shiver ran down his spine.

No, they would never be content.

But he knew his duty. He must marry and secure the title for future generations.

Thinking back on the women he'd associated with this season, none fit the role of the Duchess of Edston. Someone raised in society, with the demeanor of a duchess. Someone who wouldn't entertain more than necessary. Someone capable of entertaining herself. These requirements ruled out both Miss Gibbon and Isi.

But maybe by marrying Miss Gibbon, he could avoid socializing. She could make appearances. He could stay home.

When he entered the parlour, he stopped, his feet going cold. As if conjured by his thoughts, Miss Gibbon sat on the settee. His mother occupied the chair across from her.

"Oh, Jonathan, wonderful. Do join us." His mother waited until he forced himself to step inside and sit on the chair beside her.

"Miss Gibbon was just extending her invitation for us to attend the ball her family is hosting in a few weeks' time."

"An end of the season bash."

"One last hurrah." His mother grinned and clasped her hands. Even her happiness was light and dainty.

He shook his head as his thoughts turned to Isi and how outspoken she could be.

"You won't be able to attend, Your Grace?"

He glanced up at Miss Gibbon who watched him with furrowed brow. "No. I mean, yes, I shall attend. With mother, of course."

His mother eyed him and then cast a pointed glance at Miss Gibbon.

Holding in a sigh, he said, "And I hope you shall reserve the first dance of the evening for me, Miss Gibbon."

"Of course, Your Grace." Her eyes lit up, her smile growing. "Wonderful. We look forward to hosting such a fine family." Miss

Gibbon rose, and Jonathan and his mother followed suit, seeing her out.

"How was your drive in the park?" asked mother when it was just them.

He opened his mouth to reply, to tell her everything that had transpired between him and Isi, before he realized he couldn't confide in her. No one need know of his infatuation with an actress. He needed to move on, and it was time he chose a wife.

"It was good. It gave me time to think of the future. What do you think of Miss Gibbon?"

"She's a fine young lady from a wonderful family. I imagine she'll make an excellent match this season." She eyed him, and though he knew she wanted confirmation that he intended to make that excellent match, he smiled and nodded.

In view of society's expectations of him, Miss Gibbon had much to recommend her, but Jonathan wasn't ready to propose marriage yet.

Chapter 17

AFTER THEIR FIGHT IN the park, Isi knew His Grace would be scarce. She threw herself into her work. David had given her the part of Helena, and she'd thanked him profusely.

Before many of the others had even received their parts, she had learned half of her lines. When she knew the part by heart, she helped with the costumes that needed mending and sets that needed a fresh coat of paint or to be rearranged so they would be ready for the show. She assisted David and ran lines with the other actors and actresses.

Her father still disappeared at times but did not always return rosy-cheeked or smelling of liquor. In fact, she couldn't remember the last time she'd seen him with a bottle in his hand.

She attributed the change in him to David keeping an eye on his best friend. Something had happened to change her father's habits so drastically.

To show her gratitude, Isi volunteered to help with the production wherever she could. Between helping everyone else and practicing her part as Helena, she kept busy.

Once they began performing again, she would manage to pay this month's rent on their rooms. She would worry about next month when it came around.

The duke's patronage was a thing of the past now. Rather than resentful, she felt grateful for his assistance.

As opening night of *A Midsummer Night's Dream* drew closer, she wondered if he would be at the performance. She felt torn between hoping for a glimpse of him and hating how she pined for him.

She fretted over whether she wanted him there. Would he come alone so he could enjoy the performance or bring that woman and her distracting friends with him?

And why couldn't he have been happy for her when she'd told him she'd gotten the part she wanted? She knew playing Helena's part was right for her. She could feel it every time she delivered her lines.

The weather matched her conflicting moods as the end of May drew near, swinging wildly between warmer, sunnier days and cold, wet grey days.

Opening night arrived. Isi peeked into her father's room to find it empty. Perhaps he was at the theatre already, helping David with something. Her heart warmed at having the man she remembered as her father back again. Tip toeing past Mrs. Pitt's rooms and out the door, Isi breathed a sigh of relief once on the street. Payday wasn't for another week, and their rent was due now.

She hurried to the theatre, running lines in her head the whole way and as she helped the crew set up.

They inspected the ropes and turned, cleaned, and greased the gears. Everybody prepared until they were hungry and then took a break.

Donning her dress and waiting as her hair and makeup were done, Isi fought the urge to run and peer out from the curtain at *his* box.

As she ran through her lines again, it hit her how often Helena put herself down. Though she could be played as a funny woman, Isi realized how easy it would be to portray her self-pity as a tragic flaw. Telling Demetrius to treat her as he did his lowliest dog, pining after him when he gave her no reason to believe anything could ever develop between them, Helena was, in a way, ridiculous.

Ridiculous characters were funny, but never had she related to one. She did not consider herself a naïve young girl who would chase after a man who clearly did not want her.

Isn't that what I have been doing, though? she asked herself. She sought to please society. She performed with all her heart, chasing the most ridiculous parts, only to be rewarded with lackluster enthusiasm and lukewarm receptions from the audience and reviews in the papers.

As the realization washed over her that she allowed society to tell her how valuable she was, David came around to warn about curtain call.

Walking over to stage left, she felt her eyes glaze over. A glimpse of the empty auditorium showed that society hardly thought of her, yet she gave them too much of herself for what they gave in return.

She avoided looking up as the curtain rose on the opening act and was halfway through the scene when she had to look.

His box was empty. Her heart shattered. He hadn't come. No one appreciated her the way she wanted. Like Helena, she tried to force things that resisted.

Taking a deep breath, Isi prepared to deliver the best performance of her life, but this time, for her alone. She deserved to have someone love her. The only one left was her.

Chapter 18

J ONATHAN'S MOTHER LOOKED OVER his attire as they stood in the parlour waiting for the stable master to ready the carriage.

"Are you certain your valet couldn't be persuaded to try a slightly more distinguished knot?" she asked, pointing to his cravat.

"No, mother." He pinched the bridge of his nose. "I told you, his fingers were bothering him."

"I think it may be time to let him go. He's served this family long enough. We ought to help settle him somewhere and find a younger man to take over his duties."

Shaking his head, he adjusted the cuff of his sleeve. The man had been his father's valet from the time Jonathan was a babe in his mother's arms. Having him here was almost like having a part of his father back. Besides, the man's fingers only bothered him occasionally. Though it happened more frequently, the two of them worked around it.

His mother did not look happy, but she smoothed the front of her dress and pulled her wrap a little higher on her shoulders. "Miss Gibbon is excited to see you. You ought to speak more with the woman you intend to make your wife. Why, when she visited yesterday morning, she said the last time she'd seen you was a week ago. At a party. You seemed in a hurry to leave." She arched an eyebrow at him.

Holding his posture, Jonathan wished he were no longer a duke. He'd only attended the party to discuss with the host a bill that had been put forth in Lords. When Miss Gibbon had laid eyes on him, he'd changed his plans and left.

And that his mother spoke of his impending engagement to the girl left a knot twisting in his stomach. If Miss Gibbon or anyone else heard, they would be ruined or forced to marry.

Not that rumors mattered. He believed Miss Gibbon also expected a proposal was imminent.

He thought of the ring his mother intended to give his wife, a stunning gem that had been in the family for four generations. But instead of Miss Gibbon, his mind conjured the image of Isi smiling, the ring fitting her perfectly.

If only he wasn't a duke. The thought had plagued him for weeks. Had he not been born a duke, no barriers would exist between him and the woman he couldn't forget.

A servant entered the room and told them the carriage was ready and waiting.

He held out his arm for his mother and escorted her from the house into the vehicle. Seating himself across from her, he stared out the windows at the dark streets, the lamps casting more shadows than light.

"So where have you been hiding yourself lately? Even I have scarcely seen you."

Jonathan cleared his throat and rubbed his hands on the knees of his breeches. He was grateful for the dark interior of the carriage so that his mother could not see his face. "I had business to attend to." Let her assume it was related to his estates or his duties in Lords. He couldn't tell her, or anyone, that he'd spent much of his time tracking down Isi's father and attempting to keep the man from getting too deep into his cups.

The clip-clop of the horses' hooves on stone and the swaying carriage jarred his nerves. He'd succeeded to a point, but unless the man wanted to change, there was only so much Jonathan could do besides encourage him.

"You and Miss Gibbon will be a handsome sight. Do you suppose you will ask her for another dance after the first?"

Jonathan bit his lip to hold back the groan threatening to break free. He scratched his chin and neck before answering. "No. You know how I dislike dancing."

"But as an eligible gentleman, it is your duty—"

"I know my duty, Mother." She shrank back at the slight growl in his throat, and he mumbled an apology.

The closer the carriage came to the Gibbons' home, the more he fidgeted. The knots in his shoulders dug into his back and he attempted to stretch them in his jacket that felt too tight, though it had slid on effortlessly earlier in the evening.

Why did society expect so much? Did he not play an active role in the House of Lords? Was his estate not well tended and prosperous? How much more could they expect? Was it not enough he gave himself to the people and country he loved?

His mind raced as the carriage halted and rocked the movements of the driver climbing down.

Across from him, his mother sat, waiting. She cleared her throat, and he shook his head and exited, holding his hand out to help her.

If society could not see what a jewel Isi was, couldn't he help them by elevating her to the rank she deserved?

"Are you coming?" His mother waited, a look of amusement on her face.

He shook his head. "I don't think I am. Please give the Gibbons my regards. I've only just remembered, I have somewhere else to be tonight." He told the driver to take him to Drury Lane Theatre, then shut the door on the man's surprised face.

He gave enough of himself away. No one could dictate his choice in a wife. After all, he was a duke.

As the carriage pulled away, he watched out the window, his heart racing faster than the wheels below him.

Nearing the theatre, he saw a man pushing a cart full of flowers and rapped on the roof to indicate the driver should stop.

"Sir," he said, jumping from the carriage and hurrying toward the flower seller. "I need flowers. Please."

"Certainly. I'm afraid I have little left. What are you wanting the flowers to say?"

"Love." The word tripped from his lips.

The man smiled through his bushy beard and mustache. He picked up flowers of purple, red, and white. Then gathering a cloth and twine from his cart, he wrapped their stems and tied them. "Will this do?"

"What are they?"

"Myrtle, for steadfast, never-ending love"—he pointed to the small white flowers— "and the red and purple are anemone. They symbolize anticipation and excitement to come."

Jonathan nodded, wondering if Isi would know what they meant. Then he squared his shoulders and gripped the stems. He would make certain she knew what they meant.

The carriage waited for him, but he waved at the driver. "Go back to the ball and wait for my mother, then drive her home. I shall find my own way."

Hurrying through the last few streets, he reached the theatre and went inside. With a nod to the ushers and the peddlers selling their sweets and treats, he hurried toward the doors that led to the auditorium. He entered after a couple who laughed behind their hands. Reaching his box, he leaned forward over the balcony railing, tapping his fingers on his thigh.

Puck was conversing with another fairy about his mischief.

Jonathan settled the flowers on his lap, hoping they would still look nice at the end of the play. A stir in the air raised the hairs on his neck. Below, Isi strode across the stage. She looked resplendent in a white dress that settled just off her shoulders.

His heart hadn't had time to settle down to a proper cadence, and now it fluttered in his chest. The tension in his shoulders relaxed, and he felt a warmth spreading through him.

Not having seen her in weeks had taken its toll, and now he knew that a marriage to anyone else would only leave him with an empty feeling of longing. Despite her father and her career, no one who saw her on the stage could deny that she possessed a stunning talent. One that he knew was up to the challenges society would throw her way should she accept his proposal of marriage tonight.

His stomach rolled at the thought.

His eyes were riveted upon her. She seemed to glow, though he noticed a stiffness to her movements. To anyone else, it would simply appear regal or frustrated, depending on what her character was professing at the time. Leaning on the railing, he jogged his knee. Look up, he urged, wishing she could hear every thought in his head and his heart.

Isi never even glanced at his box while she was on stage, and when she exited and the curtains closed for intermission, he stood. His hands trembled, so he clutched at the bouquet to steady them. He couldn't wait until the play ended to know if she would accept him.

Chapter 19

ISI PACED ON THE stage behind the protective covering of the curtains, muttering her next lines to herself. She didn't need the practice. Forgetting her lines wasn't possible at this point. But it was a habit she couldn't break from past performances.

Her father stood in the wings, watching her. He didn't sway on his feet, and earlier, she smelled only a stale hint of spirits. She knew David was to thank for her father's relative soberness.

Turning, she bumped into someone holding a bouquet. Isi looked up, and her breath caught in her chest.

His Grace stood before her. He cleared his throat. "I'm sorry."

"For what?" her brow furrowed, and she studied him.

"For everything I said in the park. You were right. Helena has the most potential for laughter. And she is courageous to stand up for and chase after what she wants." He swallowed and held the flowers out to her. "I know we don't have a lot of time—"

"The curtain will go up any second." She glanced around as people took their places.

"Please, just another moment. I'm sorry for not being there these past weeks. For arguing over something so inconsequential. All it comes to is that I love you." The words hung in the air between them, and Isi glanced from his face, to the flowers he held, and back again.

The curtains swished aside, and she felt the hum of the audience die as they stopped to stare at the stillness of the stage.

She could hear them asking, *why aren't they doing anything up there?*

"I love you, and I want you to marry me. If you'll have me," he said, louder now, holding out the flowers to her.

Whispers broke out across the theatre, but she kept her attention on the man in front of her.

"You love me?" A smile broke free, and she reached for the bouquet, her fingers brushing against his. Instead of letting go, his other hand cupped hers and pulled her closer.

"More than words can say."

"You want to marry me?"

He leaned until their heads touched and said, "If you'll have me. I know we'll have people to convince, but I no longer need convincing. Without you, my life would be an endless night devoid of stars. You are my sun. My world is, and always will be, centered on you."

Isi closed her eyes and placed a hand on his arm to steady herself. Goosebumps slid over her neck. She breathed in his scent, warm with a hint of oranges, and felt as though her chest would expand forever, her heartbeat quickening. "Yes," she breathed out.

"Yes? You'll marry me?"

Chuckling, she leaned back and opened her eyes with a nod. His twinkling eyes held her in place. He leaned forward, one arm wrapping around her waist and pulling her closer.

His lips were soft and full on hers. She closed her eyes and reached for him, deepening the kiss. She ran one hand along his lapel while the other still held the bouquet being crushed between them. He tilted his head and swept his hand up her back to rest on her neck.

A moment later, though she felt like days had passed, Isi pulled back, her cheeks reddening as she heard applause.

Looking out over the crowd, she noticed most were on their feet. Jonathan was right—many would question their decision to marry. But in this moment, society accepted them.

Isi smiled and turned to face the audience, grasping one of Jonathan's hands in hers. "Take a bow," she said, as she curtsied.

He snorted but complied, bowing beside her. Giving her hand a squeeze, he said, "I'll see you after the show." Then he darted off stage. She handed her bouquet off to her father, who gave her a lopsided grin with a sparkle in his eye, and then she began the second half of the play, marveling at the parallels between her life and Helena's.

Only when Helena rejected Demetrius did he love her and win her hand in marriage. She knew the feeling as beside her, Demetrius said his line: *"It seems to me that yet we sleep, we dream."*

A glance up to Jonathan's box confirmed she was not dreaming.

As the play came to a close, Isi stood beside her father backstage, listening to Puck deliver the closing lines sending the audience back to reality. She held her bouquet in her hands and smelled their sweet fragrances.

"You love him?" her father asked.

"I do."

"He is a good man." He leaned over to kiss her on the cheek. "Not sure what I would've done without him the past few weeks. You know David was this close to letting me go."

"What does that have to do with Jonathan?"

Papa grinned and shrugged. "He's been keeping me out of trouble." With a wink, he walked away.

Turning, she saw Jonathan nearby. He stood still, his eyes gleaming as he stared at his future father-in-law. Walking toward him, she reached out a hand and brushed a thumb across his cheek, cupping his face in her hand. *A very good man*, she couldn't help thinking to herself.

Chapter 20

ISI AND HER FATHER exited the theatre, and Jonathan watched as they walk toward him. They'd needed to help clean up, and Isi had changed out of her costume.

"Have I told you how much I enjoyed your performance tonight?"

"You have. Several times." Laughing, she held her bouquet closer to her face, inhaling the scent of the wilting blossoms.

Jonathan held out a hand, and Isi gave the bouquet to her father to hold before climbing into the carriage. Jonathan urged her father to enter the carriage, and then climbed in himself. He blinked, surprised to see Isi's father sitting on the bench opposite her. Stretching, he eyed Jonathan then the seat beside Isi with a grin.

Taking the seat next to her, Jonathan smiled in the dim light.

Her father groaned and then covered his mouth as he yawned. "I don't know how people do this. Stay up all day, working. Think I'll take a nap." Leaning back in the seat, he crossed his arms over his chest and closed his eyes.

Jonathan reached his hand out, feeling his way along, intertwining his fingers with Isi's.

"You were fantastic tonight."

"So were you."

Hearing the grin in her words, Jonathan closed his eyes for a moment as a peaceful feeling settled over him.

"Did you mean it?" she asked with a hint of uncertainty.

Jonathan squeezed her hand before letting go and sliding his arm around behind her, pulling her close to him.

"Every word. Do you believe I would play such a cruel trick? Just walking on stage, I thought I would fall to pieces with the shaking I was doing."

Lowering her head to his shoulder, she breathed out a sigh. "I just had to be sure. No doubts?"

"None." He allowed himself a moment to swim in the lilac scent that swirled around her, combining with the fragrance of the myrtle and anemone flowers that were filling the carriage. Then with a kiss to the top of her head, he said, "In fact, I shall apply for a special license so we can marry at your earliest convenience. I intend to take you to our home as soon as the run of *A Midsummer Night's Dream* is through."

A quiet snore carried across the carriage from his future father-in-law, and Jonathan wondered if the man were sleeping or giving him and Isi an almost unchaperoned moment.

He felt her sit up and turn toward him. Her hand slid up his chest and rested on his cheek. Her thumb caressed his bottom lip, and his arms wrapped around her as she leaned forward and rested her lips on his. He felt her chest meet his and the pounding of their hearts mixed as his fingers came up to entwine in her hair.

She pulled back and slid her cheek along his, her fingers running over the nape of his neck, raising goosebumps. "I'm glad this isn't a dream," she whispered in his ear.

"Me too," he whispered, turning her to face him and kissing her once more.

If you enjoyed Jonathan and Isi's story, please consider leaving a review. Reviews help readers feel confident they can take a chance on a new author's books.

Also sign up for Elizabeth's newsletter to receive info on new releases and other fun!

Acknowledgments

If you are reading this, we are friends now. You are my kind of person. A person who enjoys reading the author's acknowledgments pages. I hope I don't disappoint. A ridiculous notion, because if you are reading this you probably just finished reading Isi and Jonathan's story and if you finished that, I'm guessing you enjoyed it. At least I hope you did. So there shouldn't be any pressure. I'm rambling now, but if you've made it this far, thank you. Like I said, you're a great friend.

Thanks to my parents. You never scoffed at my dreams of becoming a writer or told me I should search for a more secure career path, just in case it didn't work out. You are the best parents a fledgling author could ask for. Thanks to both my sisters who have read my stuff whenever I've asked. To the rest of my family, my siblings, cousin, aunts, uncles, and my in-laws, I appreciate all your support. You are the best tribe a girl could ask for.

My husband found me when I wasn't even looking and I'm forever grateful he did. He taught me everything I know about love and I treasure every moment I get to spend growing a life with him.

I'm grateful for digital author communities. When we lift each other up, we lift ourselves as well. To my friends at 365 Writing Challenge, I could not have done this without your encouragement.

My editor, Emily Poole of Midnight Owl Editors, helped polish this story so it shines and was a joy to work with.

Lastly, I need to thank my babysitter, Anna, who played with my three young boys a few hours a week and gave me some much needed time with my characters. Me and my imaginary friends are forever in your debt.

About the Author

Elizabeth Ann Heath is a proud boy mom who fills her nonexistent spare time writing regency romances. She lives with her husband, three boys, a dog named Koda, and a few chickens in the suburbs, but dreams of moving the entire lot, house and all, to a five acre homestead.

Liz decided she would be an author at 12. Her options were to be an architect, an author, an actress, or a dog breeder. After realizing she loved the alliteration of her first three choices, her decision was made. Though she enjoys reading a variety of genres, her favorites are historical kissing books, so that is what she writes. Liz's one regret is that her middle name does not end with an 'e.'

You can connect with Liz and find more information and updates at
elizabethaheath.com